T0064166

In the
Shade
of a
Dark
Cloud

In the Shade *of a* Dark Cloud

THIRU WARAN

PARTRIDGE
A Penguin Random House Company

To order additional copies of this book, contact
Partridge India
000 800 10062 62
orders.india@partridgepublishing.com

www.partridgepublishing.com/india

Contents

"I always think about this day. I've imagined this day, a million times in my head, on what I'll say and what I'll do, when every step I take leads to a failure. and every time I think about it I try not to remember the details and start hoping for a better outcome of an eminent situation.."

I was a typical urban city kid to whom life was enjoyable but never easy, asif was a rich playboy material, bharat a guy who never tasted success.. and she was the mystery girl who breathe the life in me.

The world is not perfect. everyone's life is broken, in one way or the other. but you will find something good for you they say, but what will you do when life strikes you down whenever you try to get back up?? Will you let it all go and let life take its toll or will you try again and hope for a better result.

The hope is there the sun is always there on the horizon or is it??its just not meant for some as life doesn't have a fairytale ending....

Preface

This book is written, in an attempt to express the days inside the so called 'prestigious' education institutes. The instances that have occurred in this book has happened, rather is still happening in real life. But, the instances may or may not have happened in my life. Even if I said that it has, then I would be very far away from the truth. So, put yourselves as 'Waran' and be apart of his journey of seven hundred and twenty days. And, please do tell me...... What would you have done if you indeed were Thiru waran????

Back where I belonged

Bangalore, india. the date was the April 3rd 2014, I was very excited as I reached anand roa circle, a busy bus station, located in the south of the city and is well known for the traffic jams which sometimes take hours to clear out, during the peak hours of the day. the big old pendulum clock in the center of the bus station struck 6.00 am, I was waiting for one of my puc friend bharat to arrive in b'lore for a month stay to undergo a CET crash course along with me in a reputed tuition centre. I was waiting near the terminal for his bus from hubli, a small city located in north karnataka to arrive. As expected the bus was late, even though I knew that something like that was bound to happen, I wanted to make sure that I reached their in time as he was coming to bangalore after 6 years and also he travelled alone, and I didn't want him to feel alone and make him miss his home on the very first day he arrived, as that was my feeling in hubli, north karnataka. the time was around 6.30 when I got his call "hi man!! I reached b'lore where are....??" before he could complete the sentence "on your left!! I yelled standing behind him after recovering from my shouting surprise, Bharat was very glad to see me it had been a long time since I had seen him and Asif. The last time I saw them was at hubli junction, when I was leaving hubli after the completion of my boards.

We reached my place around 7.45 am and the sun began to show us its warm presence. The whole journey of an hour, was pleasant. With the morning breeze hitting our face. "Hi aunty how are you??" Bharat said as he greeted my mom who was eager to see him after a long time as she always thought he was one of the very good, descent and innocent guys from school. "How was your travel and did Waran, pick you up on time??" my mom asked him and was looking at me with those mom stare. "yes aunty he did!! He reached well before the arrival time aunty…. And I am sorry for such inconvenience." Bharat said with the guilt of waking me up soo early. "relax man I am the one who gave you the idea of joining in bangalore for your CET course." I said and picked up the luggage and went to my room. we chatted there for about half an hour on various aspects of the universe and finally decided that we will head to forum, a mall in the centre of the city and attracts huge crowds as the mall attracts beautiful girls and the beautiful girls attract the boys. it gathers a huge crowd during most times of the year. "dude b'lore chicks are hot!" said bharat as he was checking out a girl who appeared to be in high school or so "yes bro I know!!" I said and continued to do the same. "I never really thought that I will live to see this day man." I told him and we were fixed on ogling at random girls. the day came to an end with finishing some yummy slices of pizza. But just because the sun goes down doesn't mean that the joy and fun should end right? After all we did finish the terrifying 12th boards. so we decided to watch some series online. "have you seen the series 'Sherlock' its aired on AXN??" I asked bharat as I was going through the list of top aired shows. "No idiot I don't even know that it existed" he replied still going through the list. "wanna see it?? It is awesome…" "we are jobless anyways, just put that up!!" he said and fell back on the bed after watching three episodes of season one he was totally addicted to it.

"Bro that was awesome!!! How did I miss it for such a long time??!! I didn't think it will be this good." Bharat said as his excitement could be made out from a person living in the next flat.. "yes it is. You have officially been sherlocked!!! And bro what did you expect a middle aged women who appears like a rhino with big eyes with black mascara around them, and to shout at her daughter in law??" I was eager, for his answer. "yeah bro I've seen that serial, my mom watches it. I feel like breaking the television's screen every time I look at that face!" he said with a wide grin on his face. "dude I don't think the producers will themselves watch such epic serials." I taunted back. It was around 1.00 in the night, and we continued watching the shows with the top ratings. "so how do you feel bro?? back home again back to b'lore yeah??" "feels good and also feels different and it is not yet over still have to get our board results and then we have to wait for CET rankings and shit like that." "fucker!! Do not talk about that!!" he said with his typical icy cold stare. "Say something on what you actually felt in those years, you never tell that to anyone properly." "It was crap and don't think about it it's over now right??" I said and tried to bring some other topic up. "what about your girl then how is she?" I asked him with that look your best friend gives you when you talk with your crush. "Probably sleep….." "Chill don't explain things in explicit detail." I interrupted him yet again. "ok!! But I don't care!!" I was stunned by his remark and thought it was better on not commenting further, even though bharat doesn't expose his emotional side to people. I knew that he really loved the girl he was dating. "what about Amrita, you don't think about her now? Because 'its over'??" the sarcasm in his voice, could easily be picked up. "I do bro I think about her a lot, but there is nothing much that I can practically do about it right?!" "wow!! I am going to stay with a practical person now for a month. It's just that I know you very well man, we spent two years of jail sentencing together you can really tell it you know" "I totally agree….. holy crap! our pre-university college life was more like serving a jail sentence. and I miss her, it is that obvious!! and it kills me to know that I can never see her again after CET." "I am not into the whole love drama but she is by far the best thing that happened to you in these past two years." bharat said as he was going through some summaries of the top aired shows. "stop talking about it man, you make me miss her more and also I don't think about it much." I said and clicked on the episodes of grey's anatomy. you don't think about it?? really?? you forget shit like that, so easily?" his eyes were still fixed on the laptop screen. "then why the fuck can't you sleep in the night???" "no clue!! Maybe I just got used to the sleepless nights now. At least we don't have to prepare for those suresh-sir-special exams." we burst out laughing, I always find it interesting that we our self laugh at things which one's terrified us.

"yes dude cause every time I close my eyes in the night I feel like I am preparing for those suresh-sir-special tests and my body is getting canned by him after the results were out."

"dude my thoughts haunt me in the night man!!! We might have PTSD?? Don't you think??"

"I felt like ghost rider when our princi, made our parents sign the deal."

"yeah bro!! the deal was signed because we actually flunked in 11th grade man!" I told him, and waited patiently for the video to buffer.

"we both know how that happened, well me it's a whole different story. I was not bothered by it!! But you!! you needlessly left Bangalore and joined that central jail."

"it was not my choice. the whole thing was a huge mess! Right from the usual family drama and emotional blackmail to get me into that hell hole, to the part when I actually climbed myself out"

"myself out?? Without your precious Amrita, you would still be down in some deep dark corner in that same hell hole." he told me with a huge evil grin.

"dude! Remember the part when I told you to not to talk about her??"

"hey!!! I just told the fact man. I always tell you this 'don't be a complete asshole' remember??" the irritating smirk on his face grew wider.

"yeah ok! Agreed. but still dude, the things we went through in that jail man. It's memorable!"

"I am forced to agree with you for a change.. I am sure you still think about it..the whole mess of a journey."

"how can I forget man? I have got the wounds of war on me!!" I said and should him the bruises on my knuckles and shoulder.

"well nice design!! Do not forget, I have an, artistic paintings on my back as well. by the great artist suresh. and I am sure neither of us are going to sleep anytime soon, so instead of sitting in front of the laptop, you can might as well tell me about your whole 'journey'. Bharat always had a sarcastic smile when he said the word 'journey'.

"well there is a popular saying that "one does not change by the destination he reaches, one changes by the journey they take.. and our journey started with a bang yeah??? The date was……."

How the end, started

The date was 15th june 2012, my first day in V.N.C and also my first day in Hubli, north karnataka. I was the new guy in town, and alike any new people. I was anxious, excited and disappointed. I was anxious and excited, because I was in a new place, a completely new environment. I was sensing the beauty of the place. Hubli was a small city, covered in lush green habitat. Only a part of hubli was occupied, whereas majority of the land was un habitat. I was not in particular of the shy types, but was always hesitant to speak with the new faces. At the same time, I was disappointed. Because I was the only one, to sit alone in the third bench. Everybody in my class, were high schoolmates and they started to form a group of their own friends, and started to get along with each other. The remarkable point was that, even though, I was sitting in the third bench, random people started to fill the benches in front of me and behind me. I felt like a total stranger, I had that sick feeling of being lonely. The first introductory class was about to start, when a tall, lean guy, with wheatish complexion, and curly oiled hair. wearing spectacles with thick frames, took a seat beside me. Mostly because every other bench was filled. He introduced himself as abhishek, and he had a high pitched voice. And took a one minute gap, before starting his next sentence to speak. There was a particular way he used to speak, it was as though, he would think a hundred times before saying a complete sentence. Even though abhishek, appeared to be too calm and composed. was a classic example of people with multiple faces, which I came to know later on. The first intro class was given by professor suresh, he was the CEO of V.N.C and he was a man truly who made a name for himself. He started out by teaching a small group of six students in his small one bed room apartment. After many years of struggling and earning a name for himself. He started his own tuition centre, which was a run away hit. It was almost an untold tradition for every tenth grader in hubli to join his tuitions, so they would get into science stream. Unlike many other countries in the world. In india, for a regular student to become an engineer or a doctor. He must get a percentage of above eighty in the 10th grade board exams in order to get into a reputed pre-university-college and get into science stream. And at the end of 12th board exams, they start up with the entrance exams like the CET(common entrance test) to get into either medical or engineering field. Professor suresh, was a typical math professor. He was lean, tall with well oiled hair. He always wore a purple shirt with black bell bottom pants. And had a sadistic look on his face. He was a very serious human, I wondered if there will ever be a smile on his face. his hunger to get 100 % pass percentage defined him.

In the last class of the day. I met ram sir, more like a trickster spirit. And was a chemistry lecturer. In the first day of class he distributed some study materials of inorganic chemistry, and informed us about the test he is going to take the next day. "Hmmmm! you all will be wondering why I gave you the study materials without teaching you anything. You all have to go through it once, then and only then you can understand my class." he told us in his pan filled mouth. He had a weird habit of lifting both his shoulders simultaneously and would twitch his head to his right shoulder. As the days passed by, I tried to get along with others. That was when I realized that, Hubli had got some tough crowd. The people were not the most, friendly or the welcoming type. According to them, I was a big city kid. And Hubli was a small place, which made me a clear miss fit. My way of living was completely different from theirs. It was soon difficult for me to handle the change. Gradually I started to miss Bangalore, the place where I was born and brought up, the place where I spent ten years of schooling in. People here, were hesitant to talk to me, they started to build complexities against me. Few even said that, they hated my presence and felt that I was stranger invading their land. Although I was a complete stranger to many. I had one real friend, that I could count on. His name was Asif, a total rich playboy material. It was in the lunch break of the first introductory class, when Abhishek introduced me to his high school body Asif, a tall fit guy, who liked to visit the gym a lot. With straight hairs that covered his forehead. He was the son of power and privilege. Ever since the beginning of first year, he had a fan following of pretty girls, who would practically faint, if he waved at them and said a 'HI'.

It had been six months, I was still pretty much a stranger. Every living soul in my pre university college was preparing really hard for the half yearly.

"our school management is treating us like robots! I mean we just wrote a test, a week back. And a re-test because we flunked in it." Asif said, and was waiting patiently outside the exam hall.

"dude, by flunking. It is V.N.C level failed. They give us a day and half to prepare for a 100 mark paper. And they have the audacity to keep the passing mark very well above fifty percent!! This is some unfair shit." I said while mugging up some equations in physics.

"bhai (brother) many are not from hubli, and are staying in P.G's or hostels. They are home sick and want some rest. We want some fucking rest. What's worse is the Sunday special classes man, I feel like I am stuck in time." asif made some last minute preparations.

"how many exams do you think we would have written in six months?? Around fifty plus?"

"we wrote a test almost, once in every three days. So it would have crossed sixty plus at least. I am not sure…. And waran, all the best bhai!" he said and rushed into the exam hall, while I slowly inched my way to my exam hall.

I felt as if, I was the merchant of bad luck. However, I tried to clear all the subjects in my exams, I would always flunk in one subject. That would award me an all expenses paid trip to the princi's chamber, where pain is a complimentary gift. slowly I was convinced that, if I stayed longer in hubli, I was sure to loose my sanity. My first year of PUC was by the definition of the word 'miserable.' All I ever wanted was to get back to bangalore. But there was only one slight problem, my parents won't approve of it. My parents as any other typical orthodox indian parents, thought that I was an over pampered kid, that refused to go to kindergarten. Eventually my cried for help, was nothing more than a tantrum. The only reason why I was able to pass the first year, was because of the deal offered by my princi which I and my parents were forced to sign. The deal stated that 'if your ward, fails to improve his/her performance in the second year of PUC. And fails to get the required percentage of marks in the two preparatory board. He /she will not be given the hall ticket to appear for the board exams at the end of the academic year.' I felt like signing away my life, which I did.

2nd year of P.U.C

The start of 2nd puc was relaxing. Me, Asif and Nashi, a guy that was thin as a stick with over combed hair. formed a group of our own. In every typical classroom, there are the last benchers. That have some epic timing sense and killer sense of humour that annoys the lecturers. Unfortunately, me and Asif, were the back benchers, and passed on many comments during lectures, which gets us fucked a lot. While still getting adjusted to life in a new place, I always used to keep an eye on Amrita. she was the girl with amazing features, her assets used to make me go "gagagaga". Ever since first year, since I first saw her wearing a green t shirt and a tight black jeans which made me love watermelons like crazy. I used to stare at her, during the lectures. But never had any courage, what so ever. To go and start a conversation with her, even though I used to stare at her since the first year, sometimes I would man up to go and speak to her, and every time she see's me going towards her direction, her eyes meet mine. I could feel my heart beats get faster, and I would walk right past her. Leaving her with a big question mark on her face, and a faint smile on her pink strawberry lips. Although, I was sure that she caught me staring at her, this time. She didn't react in the way I expected her to, I was expecting her to report me to a lecturer, who will insult me in front of everyone, After thrashing me. rather she had a nice smile, on her fair complexioned face and later waved at me. "god.. is this really happening??or did I enter my first stage of hallucination?" I thought to myself, she is like the girl with the perfect body with curves at just the right places. She was the persona of the word 'beautiful'. And I was still the guy in town, with sebaceous hypotrophy, that made my nose look alien. as every guy's fantasy, I also wanted to date her, maybe that was the normal teenager with raging hormones in me that was talking.

It was that time of the day again, it was time for the CEO to take his lecture. It was much like a storm that approaches the herd of helpless cattle. he was a textbook indian math teacher, who believes in the traditional 'spare the rod and spoil the child'. But the way of his teaching was questionable, in his classes the math geniuses continue to get better at math and the people who sucked at it, continued to suck at it. Somewhere, in his journey from a poor math teacher to a rich CEO of the pre university college that has one of the highest ever recorded pass percentage in the state, the math teacher in him was outgrown by the successful businessman that he had become. After a few weeks of teaching us, he separated the entire class, based on whom he felt were the good students. Me and Asif were in the lowest of the order. I was in the 'B' division when the things unfolded in front of me. But more or less, another person was in a similar situation, his name was Bharat.

During the time around april 2013 Bharat (or 58 as me and asif call him) had the worst eight days of his life. (Little did he know that the storm was just starting to build up) it was all he had to prepare to write his 1st year re-exam. And the kick in his balls was that he had to write the 2nd year cyclic tests side by side with his preparation. Otherwise, our beloved princi wouldn't have given his year re-exam hall ticket. Amidst all of these his family conditions worsened him and they mentally tortured him. According to them, it was completely his fault. They didn't consider throwing him in the hell hole, against his will had nothing to do with it. that's the thing about indian parents, if their kids have their own way of doing things it is always wrong in front of their eyes. Bharat, like any other average 10th grader in Hubli, was a student of Suresh sir's tutorials. Where he had a hellish experince because of CEO and Anand, CEO's right hand man, that takes care of his tuition administration. In his tuitions, they cared only about their name and fame, and didn't care much about the students school performance. They used to keep 'important' tests in tuitions, when the students had important exams the next day in their school. As a result Bharat's school performance dropped and this caused his mother to worry a lot. Not realizing that she had a part to say in his present condition..

He did manage to pass the re exams, but only with the help of a friendly invigilator. And the 'deal' which his father was forced to sign.

Vacation exams and the after-math

"Hi waran!! All the best for your exam." I heard a sweet feminine voice to my right hand side. I saw her, she was looking at me. Her eyes that smile for her was looking at me, her strawberry lips were wide. She was just a feet away from me. "ooh wow! She knows my name." I thought to myself, my heart was pounding against my chest. "hi… thanks a lot. Hope I pass in math this time." I stood like an idiot. She was still looking at me, her smile didn't seem to die out. "ok. Did so did you prepare well?" she asked me with her hypnotic voice. "fuck!! She is actually in a conversation with me. What should I say, what should I freaking say?" my mind started going blank. "well I did prepare, but not sure how the things will work out. What about you?" I said and tried to keep a descent smile, pasted on my face. "I didn't prepare well. Hey listen, I got to go now. I am sure you will do well." She kept her hand on my shoulder. "see you later then.. and all the best for the exam." I told her, and watched her walk away from me, there was elegance in the way she walked. "fucker!! What I saw, was true? Or did I get hit by a truck on the way to this hell hole? And this is some weird version of hell." Asif shook me up, and was astonished by what he had seen. "I am not sure bro...not sure at all." I said and walked into the exam hall. The exams went well, there was a lot of team work done. And we ensured everybody, would pass in it. The paper was tough, as we had expected. I felt like I was drifting of into space. It was the first good day I had, in over a year.

After three long days, of so called vacations I was eager to see my friends and also to speak to Amrita, the proportions of my eagerness varied. The date was june 10th, I was late for my college and got a place to seat in the last bench and as usual I started to check her out, and this she knew very well and I guess it was a nice way to pass the time for both of us.

"dude did you see your chem marks??"Abhishek asked, with his usual annoying way to annoy others. "what? No!! They put up the marks on the notice board or something??" I already knew the answer, maybe I was expecting him to say something like 'no asshole, I was getting bored annoying others. And thought that I will annoy some one else. And who else is a greater joke then you in this galaxy?'. "Yes man!!go see it now!" he said with his high pitched voice. I was lost in my thoughts, "It is easy for you to say fucker." I thought to myself. Still disappointed, that it wasn't a prank. "checking out Amrita is a thousand times better than this." I thought to myself. The mystery in chemistry was finally broken, I got near fifty percent, which was quite okay for me as the question paper my college had set was in IIT/JEE level. But to my dismay it was not even close to our passing mark.. "Bhai!! I almost got fifty percent... So is it considered that I passed??" Asif asked me and Nashi with his voice down. "Dude even I got somewhere, near fifty percent. But its considered that we have failed!" I uttered those words feebly. "Who is saying that??" Nashi enquired with his eye brow's raised. "Our notice board with the princi's sign!" was my equally quick response. Week after week, we were becoming weak as the results of our other subjects arrived with a bang.

After two and half weeks of easy living. The messenger had knocked upon us, one of our college peons knocked our classroom door and gave a slip to our physics lecturer, mr.Venkata naidu. He called out a few roll numbers which included me, Asif and Nashi "arrey nana go to the principal's office and all the best raa nana." naidu sir said with a smirk on his brown tanned face. While, heading down to the princi's chamber. I noticed that all our board member's cars were parked in the corner entrance of our college. "Bro! look over there and yup get ready for a gangbang." I told to Asif and Nashi pointing at the cars parked unequally, parallel to each other. We all laughed at it but knew very well on what was going to happen inside the sex dungeon aka princi's office.

Inside the princi's chamber the stage was set perfectly for the "hunger games", inside the office it was crowded like a BMTC bus. All the board members were delighted to see me, Asif, and Bharat. During that time, Bharat was still a stranger to me. inside the chamber our beloved princi opened his drawer and took out the mark list and started to growl at everybody. It was his usual step by step procedure, "the chamber of secrets as indeed been opened." I thought to myself. "you failed in the first year. But we passed you by mistake, now you failed again how are you even ready to face the board exam??" The princi's shriek voice echoed through the big room. I was totally dumbstruck and couldn't say a single word. All the board members were waiting for my answer, which I never told. ram sir decided to keep us an entire week of re-exams which literally sucked my life out.

The princi warned me about the serious consequences I had to face if I did not perform well in my half yearly exam. "but sir I am getting good marks in bio consistently." I argued "I know that but what about math??" he said "so for one subject your making me fell completely useless." I argued yet again. "do not speak to me in that tone of voice. Or do you want me to make you understand in a better way? Which I like? Get out!!" he said with anger in his old cracking voice, and his hands on a wooden cane. "what fucking tone? I tried to be descent as possible and didn't even raise my voice" I thought to myself and walked out of the princi's chamber.

Half yearly begins and half our life ends

"Dude if we don't pass in half yearly, we are dead." I told Asif, and picked my favorite football team.

"that is obvious dude. But you are going to die anyway, if you pick this team." He said looking at the LED screen in front of us.

"fuck off!!!! My team makes the legends, yours…….. Just buy them." I was a die hard Barcelona fan, while Asif was a real Madrid fan. We always thought that our teams where the best and the other one sucked.

"Dude but seriously!! If we flunk, we are gonna get fucked up bro. And our princi was epic, 'you will face serious consequences'". Asif mimicked our princi's old cracking and shriek voice.

"How am I even going to study for it man?? The exam's starts in two days, and we are here playing fifa 2013…."

"even if we get canned by Prici and Suresh, we at least have this PS3 joint, and here we are the un defeated fifa, and call of duty champions. Fist up bro!!" his fist was held high in the air.

"Bro!….. You are optimistic to say the least."

the paper as expected was designed in a way that most of us couldn't get through it, this was because not even a single question had come from our government prescribed textbooks. I still feel this is the reason why students from government colleges top in boards, as they don't refer any other book then the textbooks and our very own posh private schools and colleges teach us from reference books like modern ABC, bosco etc. that have complex and tough questions, that have no chances of appearing for the board exams.

The first exam was physics followed by chemistry and after 2 days break we had math then followed by biology. In physics and chemistry I got descent marks in both of them, In Bio, I worked myself to get 90 percent. And math well not even one fourth of hundred. Even though Asif had helped with a few chapters, and made me understand the logic in math, which I never got. Asif had huge levels of patience, much like the lord Buddha. Before the start of the vacations, our results would be displayed on the notice board. Asif never had a look at it, according to him it was a mood spoiler. Our feeling was mutual, I was back where I truly belonged. I was back in my hometown, I was back in Bangalore. The IT capital of india, and a vibrant city With classy and friendly people. Bangalore is a place, which has something for everybody. Be it the three hundred acre, botanical garden with over thousand species of flora and a glass house for the people to sit back and relax after a tough week at work. To the adrenaline seeking junkies, that loose themselves in theme parks. From the people, who are interested in culture and history. That find themselves in places like HAL museum, that hosts the vintage models of aircraft's used over the decades. Or the younger generations that enjoy the bangalore night life, filled with disco lights and EDM's in MG road and UB city. From the people that are interested in golf and racing, to the foodies who explore the street food in jaynagar, Bangalore had everything. As the people say there is nothing more beautiful then Bangalore when it rains. It was always good to hangout with my school friends, being with them almost made me forget about my life in Hubli. Whenever I got involved in some deep conversation with any of my friends, I would make so much plans, that I would forget. I had to leave bangalore soon. MG road and Church street, was our usual hangout spot. The time used to fly when I was with them. More like, flying in the speed of light. During my short vists back home, I would never feel like going back to Hubli. It made me forget everything for a short period of time. I somehow, would pretend that I will never go back. And enjoyed every second in that small bubble, that I had created for myself. But, the harsh reality always made me fall to the ground below. After the bubble that I created for myself popped, the memories of V.N.C would rush back to me. And all of a sudden, the old shriek voice of princi will be the only voice in my head. The images of the pan stained mouth of ram sir, will be playing in my head. Sometimes, I felt like running away from my family and never go back again. I always blamed myself for not trying hard enough to convince my parents. "maybe if I showed them the scars on my knuckle, they would have cared and listened to me?" I thought to myself and boarded my 9.00 pm train to hubli. During my journey from my house to the railway station. I would try to record every last seconds of it in my head. And would play it on reply until the very moment I except the part that I have to leave home again, and it never got any easy.

Everytime when we enjoy, we feel ourselves flying out of earth's atmosphere. But after the short period of fun, it is always hard to fall face first onto the solid ground, which was exactly the way I felt. I was back in my central jail on 6th of november, the very day I stepped foot in central jail, the papers were being distributed. Naidu, Salim and Sreeni sir{also from the united arab emrites} were getting ready for the rituals, that followed. I had managed to get nearly fifty percentage of the marks, while Asif had fallen short of it, by a bigger margin. "Array nana you and your friend do vroom, vroom with your bikes ra nana!! You do skidding and wheely and THAT IS THE REASON YOU BOTH FAILED" he said screaming the last sentence so loudly that I thought he was going to smash us the very next second. "Where is your friend??Waran?? get up raa nana!!" he commanded me. "Crap this is going to be a long day." I thought to myself. "you both always roam together, always on bike...... I see you both near k.M.C ground!! then why don't you study together??" he paused before I could say anything, the wooden cane in his hand, began striking me all possible directions. "You were the most innocent student in first year raa nana what happened to you?? you are with bad influence that's the problem." he announced in front of the silent class, it was like they were witnessing a satanic ritual. The only difference was that no one was wearing black hoods that covered their face, Nor did they have candles in their hands held close to their chest. "Asif!! You are gifted with wealth ra nana. But are you using it well??" Naidu screamed at him, followed with a round of hard slaps, that was echoed through the class, there was pin drop silence. For almost I moment I thought the time froze. Only way I could tell I was in reality, was by the sound of wooden cane, that was striking asif's back and shoulders.

"what the hell bro!! he thinks I influenced you." asif said with a bright red glowing face." He never got the mark of cain, on his hands or back. "innocence in the face my boy." I replied with my tanned brownish face turned into a choclate colour one with jelly toppings. the very next period I got my math marks, which was horrible not even worth mentioning. "aaah!! Who is this?? Roll number 197?? Come here fast." CEO ordered me, his wheatish skin turning red. As I stood up, I could feel my knee shiver, my legs were going weak. I felt the ground below me tremble. He took out the cane from inside the teacher's desk. "see the marks. Tell me should I kill you or hit you till the cane breaks, which is much worse?" he looked at me, and shifted his attention on the cane, and wiped it clean off the chalk dust. "kneel down sir." He ordered me and pushed my shoulder down. "great…. It is going to be fucking great." I kneeled down and kept my head down. "instead of coming to study, you can work as a broker in janthabazar." Janthabazar was a prostitute area of hubli, he wanted me to pimp them. "answer my question…" he said raising the wooden cane. "that eager to get laid?" I felt like screaming those words at his face. "good. I knew you won't have anything to say." He said and started his artistic painting on my back, shoulders. I started to keep a count of the cane strikes, there was pin drop silence, the 'wooosh' sound of the wooden cane striking my skin could be heard clearly. after crossing the 10th strike, I lost my count, all I could feel was pain, pain of the thick wooden cane, tearing my skin. I got a cane strike on my lips as well. "get up now! go sit in your place and study well, I am doing this for your own good. And come to my office, will give you some medicine." He said and lifted me up. "no….no will take care of it………sir." I said and covered my upper lip that was bleeding, with my palm, and feel the warm blood on it. Maybe he didn't intend to hit my lip, maybe he was scared to see me bleeding on the elevated stage. Maybe that's why he stopped the canning early. Usually he used to cane us for over 15mins, depending on the strength in his arm. And would make us sit in the invisible chair, with our hands stretched till the lecture gets over. Many of the students, that received it fainted twenty minutes into the punishment. I walked to my place, and kept my head down on the bench and put some pressure on my lip. I noticed that amrita was looking at me, from the corner of her eye. She was sitting parallel to me. I could not blame her for looking at me with pity, after 2 hours of back to back action most of the people in my class where looking at me, and trust me, its one of the most excruciating mental pains you will ever come across being a student. I kept my head down for the rest of the lecture.

"HI. how was your vacations??" she said and tried to be polite, I could make that out by the way she spoke to me.

"hmmm it was good!" I said and turned away from her.

"ok. How are you feeling now?" she said and tired to look at my face. "come on look at me." She said and tried to touch me hesitantly, I could see her from my peripheral vision.

"I am fucking great!! How do you think I am?? Looking great right??" in times like that, even if the worlds most gorgeous women tries to speak to you, there is only one way you react.

"shit Waran!!! It is still bleeding……….. And you are angry, it is ok for you to be angry. But listen to me, It will be alright…. It will be." I could feel the care in her voice, I did not know how to react.

"I am sorry. and thanks, I really needed someone to tell me that." I was facing her, and still my head was on the blue steel table. And my hand was on my back.

"oh god!! There is blood on your shirt. I think its bleeding." She said and covered her mouth, with both her hands. Her friends, sitting beside her. Were looking at amrita in a weird way.

"well that is the final colour in the painting." She didn't reply, rather still kept her hands over her mouth. I could see her eyes shrink.

"chill ok.. I have been in worse, this is nothing. See I am still cool." She didn't say anything, just nodded her head, with her hands still over her mouth.

The last lecture for the day was 'free' so the classes for the day, were done. I went into the washroom and removed my blood stained shirt, it was like small patches of blood at random places, all over the half sleeved shirt. "Nice design. Suresh did it right?" I heard a cracking voice, from the last corner stall, of the washroom. It was Bharat, he was shirtless and appeared drugged. His eyes were swollen, so was his face and shoulder. "Do you like mine?" he said and turned around. His back was like, a maze of scars. "The one's that are bleeding, is the recent ones." He said while drinking a carbonated drink. "what the fuck man? It Is horrible to even look at it. You got to tell somebody! This is harassment." Bharat still continued to take small sips of coke. "somebody?? Like my parents??" he said and started to laugh uncontrollably. I began to question myself, if he had got hit on the head really hard. He appeared drugged, dejected and pale. "And what exactly do you think will happen after that?" he asked me, and tried hard to control his laugh. "our parents will fight with the management, and uh…….." "And then the matter will come to why he actually hit us that bad. And slowly the topic will drift to the marks, and our management will only show the marks in which you sucked at. And also…. There will an emotional speech by Suresh or Princi, which will include the lines 'He is like my own son, and I am doing this so that he will get a bright future. It is his age, to think that I am a villain. But after he grows up, he will realize why I did this.' And after that golden globe wala performance, our parents will give in. And trust me, they will fuck our heads, when we go home. Trust me outsider! I have known these people, since the age you hit puberty and noticed that girls have a different physiology."

He said and again started to laugh. I was convinced that he got hit on his head, so hard to make him insane. "You may think that I am insane, well I don't blame you. But a word of advice brother? Don't tell these petty matters to your parents. It is just the beginning." Even though, I was listening to the screams of a madman. There were more than a few valid points. "You might very well be insane. But hell!! You are right." I said and started to wash the bloodstains off my shirt. "All that is fine. But why drinking some carbonated juice inside a stinking washroom??" "Hmmm is it stinking?? Drink this your pain will reduce. He said and threw me the bottle of coke. "some alcohol will do the trick for me, but what's there in the coke bottle??" I asked him curiously. "coke….just drink it." He said and threw me the bottle. After drinking a few gulps, my head started to spin. Everything appeared so calm and relaxed, I could feel my heart beats get irregular. Even though I was still in pain, there was a sense of accomplishment. It felt floating on a cloud. "It is not coke. What is it?" I demanded him. "It is coke with coke…….. as in cocaine. Don't worry give it sometime to settle in. You will be fine, how is the pain bro?" "I can hardly feel it. Damn it's so soothing, I love it. I fucking love this feeling fucker. But I am never going to take it again in my life." I am not sure why I said that. "really?? I know! Moral ethics?? And cheers to a really bright future." He said and turned his back again. "God! You got to stop doing that! I can almost feel your pain, by just looking at it." I said and threw him the bottle of coke. "Is it?? Well I can't! I feel like I have accomplished something." he said and proposed a toast with the plastic coke bottle. "Now, while going out. Don't make it obvious that you are drugged. You just got torn apart in class so, It is natural for you to keep a gloomy face. So wash your face, put some water on your head. Just be normal, and I hope you are not that foolish to drive." He said walked away from the washroom.

It was a Saturday and I was waiting for my well deserved holiday. Attending lectures was much like being in the middle of no man's land and receiving heavy crossfire on both the sides. "good morning sir" we all stood up to wish salim sir who had walked into the class with a slight off mood. "those who failed in the half yearly exams get up now." he said with a stern face. "not again noo!!" asif screamed in a low pitched voice. "bro three teachers teach us a subject, so does it mean that all the three of them. Will bash us separately?? Why can't it end in a day??" I told him and got up and so did asif "specs fellow how much did you get??" he questioned me "sir 33/70" I replied expecting a war of words except that I was a wounded quadriplegic soldier. "its almost 50% not considered as fail sit down" he said "thank you sir." I was starting to make myself, comfortable in my seat. "well at least this guy did not hit the shit out of me." I thought to myself. "what about you long hair??" he questioned asif, and was looking disgusted at his hair, that covered his forehead. "sir 27/70" he replied "not even close to 50 % and growing such long hairs. get out of my class and also take that specs friend of yours along." "the fuck??" I thought to myself and got ready to leave "those who got below 50% get out now" he said most of the class came out with us. And so did Isha, Amrita's friend and also used to sit parallel to us. "As long as you are with your kamina friend naa...you will continue to get caught." She said, with a formality of smiling. "Ooh wow! you noticed the fact." I responded with a smirk on my face, just as I said that salim sir came out and glanced at me with a eyes full of disgrace which might have said "This human is useless."

Later on in the evening, we were summoned to the princi's office. where they informed us that we were supposed to sit in the library for a week or so and study the subjects in which our performance was considered low. it was finally time to go home, as I walked into the parking lot I saw amrita walking to her moppet. I could see her hip sway back and forth. "hi, what happened inside the princi's office." She started checking my face, shoulder and back for blood. "gang ba……." I paused "gang discussion" I continued "they are sending us to the library for a week or so to study. if nothing else I at least got a week off to dodge the heat." the huge grin on my face, grew wider. "that is good. enjoy your vacations then." she said with a sarcastic smile. "you know the worst part of my upcoming vacation is that I won't be able to stare at you." I said with a cheap smirk. "ooh really is it?? Don't worry just for a week." she said, and gave me a slight jab. "so you actually liked to be stared at??" "No ways just that you are descent that's why." she said in a defensive tone "innocence in the face. see you later then bye." I said and kick started my bike "bye! drive slow." I could sense a mixture of, care and seriousness. "I will" I responded, "fuuck so much care??? What will I do if she thinks of me as her brother!!!" the last part bothered me a lot.

End of days in library

It had been a month since I had left the regular classes. Everyday was the same routine, it was as though we had landed in a prison somewhere in south America, most likely the prison in panama. "and they said just for a week or so." I nudged asif with my shoulder as we where studying electrochemistry, during these times me, asif and bharat got close to each other, as they say people who serve in the same battalion are more like family then friends. as making split second decisions would change their lives. me, asif and bharat where in such a situation. bharat started to speak with me and asif as he sucked at math(just like me) and asif was the go to guy as for two main reasons first of all, he was simply awesome at math and second, nobody else was ready to teach us any shit. even though my princi used to say "if any of you have any problems regarding the subject ask any lecturer or lab teachers they will explain you." in his shriek voice. it was just a stunt to show that they are doing everything within their power to make us 'studie' better. whereas, the actual truth was that the class lecturer's where just book worms and dismissed any questions put before them if it was not from the book they teach, and majority of the teachers were under qualified and moreover had an ego so they are not under estimated by other students. "hi bro. the great bharat has joined forces with us." asif said as I entered the library and entered my attendance in the register, an old worn old. Red binded book, with red margins and double spaced horizontal ruled lines. "hey man. we are all one bro!! because the princi and CEO insulted all the three of us equally." I said and took out my chemistry study materials. "at least you escaped off after the first round of fucking.. after you left for your sister's marriage the princi called all of us again on november 14 th" asif said as he was checking out pooja, a pale white chick with ok features. "It was luck that I escaped on november 9th itself!!" I said with a sigh of relief. "because amrita started to show her care for you from that day??" asif said with an evil grin on his face "nope because I was saved from yet another utter humiliation. bro I don't care if the lecturers hit me man, it is just a temporary pain but the scolding and getting screamed at!! I just can't take it." I told asif and continued with my electrochemistry. Although I really liked to be with amrita, obviously she was the most, prettiest girl, I have seen in my life. She was beautiful, intelligent and had a wicked sense of humour. I didn't want to do anything, that will make her stop talking to me. The refuge I found, while being with her. Was like hearing to a beethoven classic in outer space. The test at the end of each day, was sucking our soul. It felt like having a colony of leeches on your body the entire time. The results, which was reviewed by our princi at the end of every week, served as a great anchor.

"Bhai I didn't study much show me ok?" Bharat asked me hesitantly. He was not the easy to get along types. "Don't be that formal just tell us what to do." I replied. The test on electro chem went well and for the next three days we had to prepare for other chapters in chemistry and it went dry and ordinary. If our voice, reached the audible frequencies. Our librarian would shout at us from his seat near the entrance of the library. "Bro he is not in his level" Asif commented "Nobody in this college is there in their level, everyone thinks that they are the boss." Bharat added. "From the way you said that I am sure you have had an episode with such people…. Tell it bro." I said as I pretended to read physics and practice the derivations "Long story man…. Leave it" Bharat said "Long day ahead." I told him pointing towards the old clock which was placed on the upper most corner of the library, and the four HD camera's that were installed to monitor us. I am not sure if ATM'S in india, are installed with such sophisticated camera's. The library was big in area, with blue and white coloured walls with cracks, due to seepage in a few corners. It didn't particularly, have the homely environment. It was as though we were walking into the casualty ward of the hospital. "okay! me and chiru bhai were hanging out in the parking lot in the 15 mins short break day before yesterday. Everything was going on in the same usual manner, then came, that useless watchman and said "Is it ur dad's bike to sit on?" It was not in his position to question me. I replied "Why you think my dad can't afford a costly bike?" The reply which he gave me really pissed him off. "By looking at your face itself I can come to know from which kind of place you come from" that bastard told me, Bharat's level of ego was not be taken easily. "I took chiru's keys and started the bike in front of him and told him to talk with more respect." "Not your bike so keep quite." He fucking said me to keep quite! I went near his face and told him to shut the hell up then chiru bhai shouted at him that if he wanted, the watchman will not see the sun set in the evening and also told him to salute every student, who parks their vehicles their and take a tip from them instead of telling them what to do, his exact words where "Thu watchman hai thu sirf watchman ich ray tho samjhe (You are just a watchman, so you better stay in your level.)" And the bastard later on reported this incident to suresh and that idiot twisted the topic into math marks and told my dad to come and meet him. my dad met him today and I don't know what will happen in my house." he completed his side of the tale. "Dude really you and Chiru bhai, threatened a watchman?!! That is like totally lame!! What do you think Suresh will tell your dad and is that why you came late today??" I asked him with ODURF{ooh dude you are fucked} smile. The very second he took Chiru's name, I know he was in some deep shit. Chiru had grown up in a tough neighborhood. That will make places like brooklyn, seem like a nursery school. The average guy in his hood was around 6.3ft tall and would weigh around 300 pounds. Chiru himself was huge built, and a hot head. Clearly he wasn't the guy to be messed with. His area was popularly known for smuggling, illegal arms dealing and drug trafficking. The law enforcement in his area, was toothless to say the least. Chiru had a heart of a kid, and a mind of a criminal. "he just put some masala and my dad blindly believed it." Bharat said with 'I know I am gone' look. "Dude everyone's dad want their children to be happy and well settled in life and due to the illusions created by people like Suresh and Ram, our parents felt it would be best if we studied here." I told Asif and Bharat. "Is that why you cry yourself to sleep like every alternative day?? Because your dad thought it was best for you to study in Hubli instead of B'lore??" Asif asked with a curious look. "He thought its better for me to join here as he was afraid I'll hang out with the wrong people and become a heroine addict if I was left in B'lore with no paternal care…." I replied trying to be cool. "And how is that working out for you??" Bharat asked. "It sucks here. I mean they don't even teach us from the textbook and they are keeping us in this library since 15 days + and I am being treated like an outer space alien and considering the fact that its been a long time, since I spoke to him. But a good thing is that I didn't become a heroine addict. I became a………… fucking cocaine addict, thanks to Bharat. So as a whole the decision to bring me here was rat shit." I said and waited for the librarian to scream at us, he didn't. Under the table, Bharat slipped in another packet of cocaine wound in a small piece of newspaper. Which I quickly hid, in between my books. There is no such thing as one time try in the world of drugs, there were two options in front of me. First one, feel the pain and the humiliations on daily basis with nowhere to go and feel the soul getting rotten inside your body. Or the second one, take some crack in and feel on top of the world. like many, I loved the second option. "If there is a raid now! Then you are dead! And anyways, the way you feel is natural, every teenage kid thinks his dad is evil and a villain, I prefer not going home early when my old man is around." Asif said, and waved at the girls sitting in the opposite end of the library, who had their eyes glued on him, most of the time. "Not exactly… For every guy when he is young his dad is his superhero and we look up to our dad. But as we turn into teens our dad turn strict so we don't get spoiled. What they don't realize is that by their old practices of disciplining their child they forget to show their love for them and also go with old methods of commanding their kid and not giving him the freedom to speak and gradually as he grows up he doesn't feel the need to even speak to his old man. So in short by doing all of that the hidden love the father has for their own kids turns into…….." "Rat shit" Bharat, completed my sentence. "And how the fuck you know that I cry myself to sleep??" I questioned asif with a surprised face although I knew that he noticed the way I keep my face dull early in every morning. "I did not.. But you got all sentimental!!! I meant it like a figure of speech." He said and tried hard to control his laugh. "don't worry man just countable number of months left now." Bharat told us with a slight hope.

It was november 27th, the date that I will always remember. This was the day, when I got into my first ever major fight with anyone in Hubli. The girl which had developed a crush on Asif, and was convinced that he was in love with her. Was hanging out with some other guy near our college. "Photo nikal bey uski(take her photo bro)" Nashi said in a sarcastic way and I just flashed my phone at them and said "Han nakal liya bhai(yup all done man.)" and stood over there and made jokes on her and that guy who she was chatting with. "He is a true product of national market" commented Asif and we all were laughing uncontrollably just when Nashi noticed that one of our juniors who happened to be that guy's friend had began a long sprint towards him and told him something.. "National market is going to come towards us" I said with a smirk on my face and like a true hero in a Bollywood movie he came towards as with his karisma zmr and parked his bike near me.. I was about to walk away when he stopped me. "Hey you!! Come seat behind me I know many hosur people!!" he said "Okay nice..But why should I come??" I said with a smirk on my face as even I had a few friends there including DK{drift knight} kiran, who could literally bash the shit out of anyone. "why did you take our photo??" he asked me with his eyes widened "who's photo?? Go ahead check my phone...... If you want to" I said and took my phone out. "Don't be over smart!! I know you took my pic with her" he said as he got down from his bike "I have a cheap micromax phone not an iPhone and also even an iPhone won't have such zoom range. Just check my phone" I told with slight fear in me and handed him my phone and typed in my long password and showed him the gallery. After going through my pics he finally said "If that picture leaks!! you won't be able to write with your hands" I stood quite. "oookay now you go from here..No tell your name and then go!" Asif said with a commanding voice "say sarkar! you will know" he said and took his bike and accelerated away.. "You don't think that he is planning to hit me right??" I asked Nashi with a slight doubt "abey kaminey if he even touchs you..I have people who can break him!!" Nashi said assuringly "Don't be scared of such punks bro. one call to my aunt he won't get out of prison." Asif said with a smirk rather an evil grin on his face.

The next day, as I left for college I was driving a bit more fast then usual and also avoided going through the hosur-unkal cross which was the quickest way to go to my central jail. After I reached the library and marked my attendance. Just then Isha stood behind me and said "Hey.. what happened yesterday??" she said in a worried tone of voice "Nothing. what happened now??"I said and pretended as if nothing had happened "Its better if you don't take fights with 6D she is very dangerous!!" she said in a concerned way. "When she wanted a punk to come and give me and Asif a trashing, Then itself I got to know her level" I said with a smirk on my face.. "Noo yar!! I heard she has told a few people from hosur to hit you and Asif." "what the fuck??!!! Really?? And when is this supposed to happen" I asked her with a bit of concern {scared to death actually because I had seen the work of rouge's from hosur and trust me it is not pretty} "End of college today be safe yar!!and did you take her picture??" she asked with an interrogative look "she is not sunny leone to have her pic in my phone" I said with a smile on my face "okay be careful….. today" she said with a smile on her face.

"bro guess what?? sarkar and 6D have arranged to hit us after college." I said nudging asif's shoulder. "fuck he can hit us. and don't fool around!" he said in a casual way "I am serious isha leaked her plan bruuh!!" "fuck you are not joking then??" he said as he stood up. "no you idiot!! we are going to get raped by hosur waala's" I said and got up, we both went towards isha and spoke to her about the detailing when chiru bhai and bharat entered the library. "hey thiru some local guy gave you a threat??" bharat asked me with his cunning, calculating eyes. "no!! Not a threat. he is bringing people to hit me and asif." I said with a total dumbstruck face "you think I'll let them hit you?? When I said that you are my friend I meant it idiot" chiru bhai said with his white face turning red "thanks man but I will handle it??" I said "by doing? what compromise with them??" bharat asked "yes by doing just that" I replied "fucker they won't even talk to you!!! they will only break your head." bharat was furious, and was ready for a fight. "let me call my people and ask about him." bharat rushed into the washroom, and made a few calls and after a while he announced that there was no one named thinku in hosur and in the short break we went into the class just to see 6D's reaction. There she was with her hands folded and her eyes determined before I could say anything, Chiru went right on her face. "you told people to hit him and Asif?? Tell them to try! I'll personally hit everyone of them." he said with his red anger striken face "No yar sarkar is not a don and all.......he is from GG college" she said by hearing Chiru's commanding voice and the rest of the day went pretty normal everyone in the college got to know the news and finally before going home I saw Amrita after a long time "Hi!!! Long time..." I said looking at her completely awestruck. "Hi thiru! Did you take that picture??" she asked with a worried face. "Nope!! I did not take any picture it was a simple misunderstanding and it almost evolved to a gang war." I said with a smile on my face, I didn't even realize when or why I started smiling "I heard people wanted to hit you and all, I thought you were in trouble." she said with her eyes which smile for her. "Nope! Got things in control! And thanks for asking me. You are one of the few friends I have here." "you are welcome, Stay out of trouble. And come down to the our class sometime na?" her eyes grew bigger as she said the last few words. I don't even know why someone like her, would say that to someone like me. "okay, I will! and I'll see you later then!! Bye." I said and started my bike's engine. I was always short of words when talking to her. "Bye and drive slow and don't do your showing off stunts." she said with a huge grin on her face. "Showing off?? It is natural talent." I said and put my helmet on. "Whatever just don't do it!" she said and walked away to her vehicle and I left my college and kept an eye on everyone who were not in the college uniforms and also had chiru bhai as an emergency stand by for obvious reason.

Hulk Smash

Luckily for me, nobody were looking to jump on me that day and after a few days of cold war between Asif and 6D things went back to normal. Me, Asif and Bharat where beginning to enjoy life at that moment we didn't have to get questioned by any lecturer that used to target us. No more torturing Suresh sir classes and no need to hear the screaming voice of Naidu sir. The last sentence didn't happen that easily and as any teenager's luck the ghost of the girlfriend's past didn't leave us.

And on the fate full day the lion entered the library along with his puppy dog sreeni, who was a lecturer in kuwait, UAE. sreeni was an extremely lean and lanky guy, with lot of pimples on his face. Bharat always describes him as a skeleton dipped in hot tar. He had a deep voice which would shock anybody who hears it after seeing his physique as a whole he was a contrast to his owner naidu. Naidu sir was a medium height, short tempered person who has the loudest voice I have ever heard. if he was taking a lecture in one class the entire floor and ground floor can hear his voice provided the class is silent. According to the hulk, I was an innocent guy till I became asif's best friend. and didn't like me joining with asif and bharat thinking they were bad influence on me, little did he know that me and asif had a metallic bond and with bharat joining us we were having covalent bonds in between us. as naidu and sreeni had walked into the library naidu addressing us as the terrorist batch to which every clerk and teacher had a smile pasted on their face. sreeni sir gave us some work to study about pn junction diode, transistor as a bitch, I mean switch etc "I didn't see you in the principle's chamber that day when we called all the students who got less in physics sir!! Where were you??" sreeni asked walking towards me "I was out of station sir." I replied and after staring at me for some time. "ok read it now" he said with his deep voice and went away.…..I was actually lucky because when every student who had got less marks where getting there ass banged, I went off to attend my sister's marriage which was around 870 kms from hubli.. and when I returned to college they directly sent me to the library {I already got to know what had happened from my C.I} I was quite happy with this as I was in no mood or condition to seat in any lecture classes.

After writing another test, everyone called it a day. when suddenly around 5.00, mr. naidu and sreeni barged in and gave us some homework to do for the next day. i had a long drive back home and was exhausted but still decided to do the home because the reason was very simple "naidu!!!!!" imagine what will happen to the mindset of a student when a lecturer such as naidu screams at them with his eyes that widen three times its actual size and turns blood red. so I decided to finish at least 7 of the given 12 questions because no matter how beat up I was I didn't want to be in the receiving end of mr. naidu's thunderous hands. after I was done with about 7 – 8 questions I decided to wind it up and thought I will finish it in the college and started to do some web chat and finally fell asleep.

Slowly, I did get adjusted. To my hubli way of life, as usual my day started at 6.30 am in the morning I managed to get out of bed with great difficulty I didn't have my sister to wake me up. the usual way she used to wake me up was by calling me repeatedly till I pick up her call. I lazily got up from my bed and was ready for yet another day in hell. While leaving to my college my mom and dad used to stare at me with at most care. before leaving my dad will always tell me to wear my helmet. dad who is usually busy with his work which required a lot of travelling, it was almost his genuine skill to make good business deals with the top most companies in the country. well he was a go to man for the job and he was in one of the highest position in his company, because of all that I never had a problem to spend cash, I could spend all I want and get my pocket money re-filled at any instant. but the downside was because his job that required travelling, I was not really close with my old man and due to the amazing episodes that had been happening with me in my life. At that time of life, I preferred not talking to him much.

"drive very slow don't cross 30 km/h." that was his exact words whenever I left for college. "sorry dad, always ride at a speed well above 85 km/h." I thought to myself and left for hell. after reaching my college at around 7.40 which was my usual time and was one of the earliest to arrive in hell along with amrita and this gave us more time to chat, laugh and stare at each other, this continued for many a days, I still didn't have any courage to ask her out. Or even ask her number. "what if I ask her number, and she asks a billion question? What if she asks for my number, and saves it has 'thiru brother' in front of me?" I thought to myself. I could hardly speak properly to her, and if she asked me any twisty questions. I was sure to get screwed up. I was surprised to see bharat, who had come early that day and I asked him about the homework the conversation went like

"bhai!! homework kiya kya (bro did you do the homework)??

"no bhai. What ever they are teaching in college itself I am not able to study from where should I do the homework??said bharat, with his worried look.

"bro if you don't do it, naidu is going to fuck your mind up and tear your ass wide open so that I can park my bike in there!! How many questions did you complete by the way??

"not even one, yet to start…how did you complete??

"I completed 7 dude did to complete around 4 questions!!" I said a bit worried.

"swastik has completed it ask him!!"

Swastik was a konkani, he was a short, spiky haired and had a french beard with a three day stubble on his face. I got the homework from him and the work process started…by this the time was exactly 8.10 when asif walked into the library and marked his attendance with his cool jacket straight long hairs and a big brown bag. seeing him pooja became nothing short of an excited atom and both of them started their innings, pooja took asif seriously but the plain reality was asif did that for fun, and pooja was not really his type. asif was a rich playboy kind a guy I knew asif since the very first day of our jail sentence. he was also from the same 'cbse' board the board in which I spent 10 years of schooling in. his dad was the managing director of a business firm associated with the tata groups. and as any rich and powerful kid his 10th percentage was low (in standards of our pu college) but because of his aunt who is a political big shot of north karnataka our principal ankalgi, immediately agreed to give the seat before which he was very reluctant to do so. during the initial days of our puc life me, asif, and abhi. were really close, as time progressed abhi even left speaking to us and we became more close to kiran nashi, asif was really good in chatting and mesmerizing girls he used to be their dreamy boyfriend until he backs out saying he was not even in search of a serious relationship. he was a heart throbber and also a heart breaker for the freshly formed females. most of my time spent in hubli was with asif. even after coming into solitary confinement {library} our level of madness didn't stop rather we used to crack some adult jokes that makes some lab personals laugh their brain's out so our days in solitary confinement was very good in a way because if we didn't go in there we would never have got to get close with bharat 58.

Although me and asif would try to get the number of each others crush. we didn't have any serious issues with it. as I never flirt with his true love and he would do the same to my developing crushes. Bharat used to tell us, that me and asif fight like wild cats (he said this when isha gave me her second number and didn't do the same with asif and our hero went into depression.) but for us chicks come and go as if they never even meet us so friendship was more important to us we even had a slogan "we ride together, we die together, we are bad boyzz forever!!" I must thank the scrip writers of the 'bad boys' series for the line.

By the time asif had finished his batting innings with pooja the old clock in the centre frame wall of the library struck 8.40. asif finally settled down in his place and I asked him the same thing which I was asking every living person from the morning "bhai homework kiya kya???" "bro!! Relax I know people like naidu they just try to scare us!! Nothing else, you have to show some balls you know! don't be a pussy." asif said in a cool way which very few people posses naturally. yeah he was one of them, no wonder girls go behind him I thought. "I know that dude!! But I don't want my balls to get cut...... no rather get smashed up by hulk. I said as I was rushing through the points on n- type semiconductors "you worry and think a lot waran!! Just try to live in the moment man!!... and did you see spoorti today?? She was hot!!

"yeah whatever man. and bro she was hot indeed...... actually I didn't feel the heat though, cause I don't want to get my fingers on her. While, you will feel the heat because you are inching your way to touch her!!" I taunted back as I was checking spoorti out. spoorti was a fair, thin and talkative girl but she lacked one thing that could have made her a hit star in our college she didn't have a "big heart" that could catch anyone's attention. "yes bro she was looking like P.C in that new item song!! and by looking like P.C, I only mean the part where she hooks her blouse." swastik added with a semi pervi grin which only guys can have on there face when they check out beautiful girls. "wtf bro?? there was something nice to see when she hooks her blouse. what can spoorti possibly show??" I commented as I was beginning to draw the diagram of a npn transistor with vengeance as any pre university course student will know what a pain in the ass diagrams can be. "spoorti's kids won't get proper nutrition bro, her husband will finish half of her storage then what will her poor kids do with the rest half??" bharat said as he was sitting calmly and worrying on various mishaps that can only happen to him in the entire world. "fucker why are you so worried man if you where her husband you would finish her entire storage and her children would be vampires as they won't have any nutrition to drink." asif said as we were laughing really loud, loud enough to catch everyone's attention "jha bey bhosdikai mai terai jhaisa harami nahi hun" (fucker I am not a con like you.) bharat said as he gave his pissed of cold eye look.

our entertainment was being done by bharat 58 and asif, I had completed most of my work and was just left with another pain in the ass diagram.. "dude I am hungry lets go out to some hotel!!" swastik suggested, and set his spiky hair right. "plzz bey I want break from this jail like atmosphere." bharat said with his pleading tone in which his eyes begin to shrink awkwardly, even I wanted to go out for the same reason and finally a bit reluctant asif joined us. we went to a hotel which was about ten minutes drive, from our central jail we somehow managed to convince the watchmen to let us go and fortunately he did.. in the hotel we ordered some masal dosa and chola batora's it was very tasty indeed one thing I like about hubli is the "saujhi" restaurants not only the girls from their part of the world look beautiful, they can cook some mouth watery dishes. It was around 10.05 am when I rushed my buddies out of the hotel but still swastik ordered some "pan" and forced me to try it. and to respect his choice I had the same. the real trouble started here.

I felt a bit heavy headed while on the way to the college "thank heavens the college is near by." I thought to myself and later I enquired swastik whether he felt the same way he just gave an affirmative nod closing his eyes and keeping his palms on his face. "bro I think you guys have drunk bhang pan" bharat said with that awesome expression our friends give when they know that we are about to get screwed. I was taken back by bharat's statement even though I felt it was a joke first but unfortunately we did indeed drink that dread full drink!! Even though I've drunk vodka and other alcoholic drinks I didn't get that effect which I felt at that moment maybe the thoughts of getting confronted by our hulk professor added to the effect.

By the time I finally got settled in our solitary confinement {library} which was filled with people as our fifteen minutes tea break was on progress and after sometime of chatting with chicks and asif was fixed on embarrassing me in front of the chicks who I was chatting with, by saying things like "waran why did you take bhang pan bro?? you should not do like that" and keep his hand on my shoulder, as if consoling me.

"bey waran how are you feeling now still hung over from that bhang pan??"

I did feel like killing him at the moment though. and finally the king arrived with his two pet dogs and what made it worse was that naidu sir was already in a semi hulk mode and he started to check our home works. "broo I am fucked now!!" was the only thing asif said "let the games...... begin!" was the voice note on my mind.

Asif was still recovering the 'memorable' moment of naidu sir checking the homework, he had clearly under estimated hulk's potential and he had that look that he is going to regret it thoroughly. In the meantime the hulk had got kiran hosumani as his victim! Even though D.K (kiran hosumani that's what we call him. He was a mad fan of the 'fast and the furious series.' Like so many of us. He had the same leather jacket and hairstyle as D.K takashi of Tokyo drift. Eventually the name stuck to him.) had come early around 9.00. he didn't start to do his homework and what added fuel to the situation was that he had failed in the half yearly with minimal marks and also he had not brought his bag to central jail, that is because in the lunch break we are allowed to go outside for food as our canteen food sucked the watchmen didn't have any issue with it unless anyone takes their bags and plan to bunk.

This was enough to unleash the hulk. Mr. naidu bent him down and gave a shot with his elbow on D.K's middle spine, he started coughing profusely, and then two slaps on the right cheek and a punch on the left!! And plucked his shirt buttons in the action of throwing him against the old white-blue painted wall. when this was going on all the lecturers and lab assistants from our floor came to see the massacre, what pissed me off was that nobody tried to even speak out and tell the hulk to stop instead they were looking at us as if they meant to say "if you don't do what we say. you will be next." I quietly went around the hulk and gave my homework to sri ram sir, I didn't complete the pain in the ass diagram. I remember the actual conversation between me and sri ram sir which was like :

Me:- "sir..please correct it!!!"

SRS:- "hmmmm why should I?? your diagram is incomplete."

Me:- "I know sir. just save me once sir please, sir just once sir please."

And luckily he did correct it. And in our country by correct it we mean just put a tick mark and sign it don't actually try to correct it, that's exactly what sri ram sir did. naidu sir saw my work and put a hugh tick on my paper.

Seeing asif standing up in the list of homework defaulters the hulk's temper was beginning to raise as he also believed that asif was the bad influence on me, but asif did keep his cool and picked a random paper from someone else's book kept on the table, which luckily had some random physics derivation, do keep in mind it wasn't even the actual homework. but because of his presence of mind naidu, couldn't do much and told asif and I quote "arrey nana!! Your parents are giving you costly jacket or as Mr.naidu used to say jaw-ket and a bike.. ondhu salaa yochinai madri (just think for a moment. Naidu sir did try to speak in kannada, but whatever he tried to say was always said in a typical foreign accent to the language.) are you worth the money spent?? Asif just kept his mouth shut and stud down after he was done with our table, naidu moved on to the parallel one where chiru bhai and 58 were standing…. THAD!!! A hugh deafening sound overcame my ears it was the sound of naidu's hands striking chiru's cheek.

"sir I agree. the fault is on my side but don't hit me." chiru said with his white pale face reddening and one could sense anger overcoming him. But there is nothing much he could have done the fault was entirely on his side this was the time when teachers where trying to pull us back in every way they could and we could not give away such opportunities. "why ra nana?? It is your fault and you agreed to it but you still have the dare to back answer me??

"sir I didn't get low marks in physics, I just failed in math I will not do your homework!" chiru said it as if getting ready to hit the crap out of the hulk.

"CHIRAG!!" Naidu screamed his throat out, you could clearly see his veins on the side of his neck "you raise your voice with the watchmen, the lecturers, the lab persons, the principal also. do you want to destroy yourself and the college?? Naidu sir continued.

"I didn't fail in physics and I won't do the homework sir, I will speak to suresh sir if you want.. and if I wanted to destroy the college it would have already been destroyed by now." Chiru bhai said with his total bad ass attitude and temper in his voice.

In all this action, Bharat who was supposed to be KIA (killed in action) survived with a little insult. naidu sir was screamed his name out. 'BHARATHHAAA' with his arms spread out and said god knows what you will be doing in that big house. to which bharat's eyes shot up mostly thinking "getting high on coke… do you want some?"

The Other Side of the Coin

Although everyone thinks of kiran hosumani as a cool dude who doesn't care about anything related to studies and always remains cool and composed. He always bunked classes, he used to escape whenever he wants, this character of him makes him eligible to star in any escape act!! But as they say every one notices the negative side of the person no one really cares about what is good in a person unless they are in love with that person or that person is incredibly handsome/ sexy or that person is dying.

It was very fine day the weather was cloudy with a cool breeze and the best about that day was that it was a holiday. it was a holiday after 14 continuous days of hard studying. bharat called me

"chutiya!! got up or no??"

"yuuup got up long back.. sup?"

"I know that you are jobless so come to K.M.C ground in 10 mins."

"sure bro!! See you there"

"since I know that you can fly with your bike and you are still in bed the 10 mins include you getting up from bed, going into the washroom and getting excited and then you start to……"

"jussst stoooop! I'll be there and asshole let me guess you are staring at a girl near by and shagging yourself in K.M.C?? oh wait did you take up the ground's white washing contract??"

"fuckkaa.. just get here ASAP."

K.M.C ground was poorly maintained but the spectator sit out was worthy enough to be called a sit-out. There, I saw bharat staring at something on his phone and kiran was having a menthol cigar in his hand. I am not sure what was so special about that day everyone was feeling light headed I am not sure whether the smoke puffed out by D.K had anything to do with it. But on that day D.K the carefree stunt hippy opened his heart out "this place is a fucking hell bro. everyone thinks they know me but they don't even know my favourite cigar brand." D.K said has he puffed out a huge cloud of thick smoke "well if you bunk 7 out of 9 classes every day and don't bring a bag to a P.U college people do tend to judge you right bro?" I said with a sarcastic smile "every fucking human being here is telling me the same thing bro I bunk I bunk I bunk!!" D.K said almost irritated.

"I think the hard fact, that you do bunk like a pro has something to do with it." I said with my smile turning into a laugh "everyone tells that I bunk classes but nobody bothers to know why?" he said clearly irritated "have you said it before bro?" bharat asked with his worried eyes and shrunken face still staring at his phone. "sasha grey quit the porn industry??" I nudged his shoulder "fuck you man. We will have our 1st preparatory in jan first week it seems." bharat said with a worry "it is just December, now bro and stop worrying this much. aaah is it official is it a text from our college??" I said still keeping my cool. "nope swasti sent it to me." "then fuck it and listen to kiran!!" I said looking at D.K who didn't give a fuck about our conversation. "I only bunk because of the pressure on me rather the pressure put on us I can't handle being targeted every period of everyday by every teacher. I actually admire you bro" D.K said looking at me with seriousness in him teary puppy like eyes. "you thought me how to stunt bro that's the only thing I am enjoying in life at the moment and why do you admire me bro??" "you don't run away from problems bro you stand and fight" "correction by fight you mean getting punched repeatedly." "whatever the fuck you do!! You keep your cool. but I am sure that deep inside you will be thinking about it a lot."

"yes I do.. but I want some credits for my sufferings I just move forward because I have no choice" "had you been given a choice would have you chosen to fight" bharat said finally after moaning over his future failure vision.. I didn't answer him. "I don't have any reason's to stay and get fucked up rather I'll spend my time on the street" said D.K as he finished his cigar "my family thinks Iam good for nothing and they don't give shit about me or what I want so I don't care about them" he said as he crumbled the ember of the 1/4th cigar that was left with his foot. "all you are doing his proving them right bro!!" it isn't much of a choice do whatever your parents say irrespective of whether it is actually correct or a hypocritical way of our parents testing us to see if we listen to them without back answering them otherwise you are a bad guy." said D.K

"bhai!! Welcome to india. Bharat commented with a smirk on his face. I do agree all our parents to their kids to grow up and be happy and stuff but majority of such indian parents throw their kids in such institution which has a high reputation of being strict and getting a very good pass percentage, they throw us in there so that we don't indulge our self in bad activities and end up like low life guys who live on the street. but they failed to see the pain we go through every day and think of it as tantrums but the worst feeling is that a few parents can actually see their child going through hell and still think of it has every 12th grader has been going through the same since ages but times have changed now. It is no more a student –teacher relationships in these institution it's a master-slave one. go against whatever they say and then your whole life is screwed." I said staring at the wide barrel ground the weather had become more pleasant it was slightly drizzling. "that's why many sexual harassment cases go unreported not only in small towns but also in these prestigious institutions." bharat said with his clearly irritated face, whenever our beloved bharat 58 gets irritated (by whenever I mean most of the time) his eyes shrinks small his upper lip opens up exposing his white teeth, and his voice gets into a higher pitch.

"bro this hard fact fucks me the most!! Our dad and mom see us going through hell and after countless fights with them they will be thinking of freeing us from the jail sentence, but at the same time. they think these jails actually help us get a life because of the illusion created by our prestigious institution. They don't realize we become robots with no feeling and at least many didn't have any feelings in leaving them behind in an old age home in pursuit of their ambition and live life. "BRO!! WAIT UP!!" bharat interrupted me. "isn't that what ram sir told us?? His exact words were 'follow your goal only don't care about your friends, parents and your happiness follow your goal.' kiran gave an affirmative nod as he released a long puff of smoke from his third cigar of the day. "the whole point of keeping a goal in life is meant to give you happiness right??? what good is a goal achieved when you have nobody including your parents to be happy with?? I said still staring at the heavens above the dark heavy rain clouds along with the sun gave a beautiful orange sky, which used to make me feel like I was in mars since I was a kid. "moreover if naidu sir wasn't our lecturer, and if he was just a common man on the road he would have been booked for attempt to murder after the way he hit you that day!! I continued saying and pointing towards D.K. "if he wasn't our teacher kiran would have killed him then and there." added bharat. that is partially true, as kiran was a hot head like so many people in hubli and I have never seen him take shit from anyone. he used to hangout with the meanest and baddest people. He had close contacts, with a 35year old local don in hosur a well reputed area in hubli, for its underworld. if any problem happened to us like a fight over a girl or fight because of a girl, D.K was our go to man. just because he played the body guard role, didn't mean he was our a pawn for us. We respected him for what he truly was, he was a nervous kid who couldn't stand being targeted and didn't have anyone to go to in his time of desperations. Everyone has a talent, and for kiran it was racing. he is the best racer and drifter I've seen in my life till know indeed he was a DRIFT KNIGHT a.k.a D.K that's what he used to call himself.

Annual Day of V.N.C

It was the annual day of our central jail, and it was held in a new venue for a change instead of the usual SG hall where suresh sir used to keep the passing out party for the 10th graders in his tuition. he had kept our annual day in R.N shetty concert hall and as planned me, asif, and nashi but on that day my bike didn't start at all. I tried to get it up and running for about 15 mins but I couldn't even hear the pre ignition engine sound and as we were late we decided to make the trip on asif's bike and nashi moppet we thought it wasn't a good start, people do believe that if you are about to take your vehicle out and it doesn't start it's a bad omen (the actual problem might be things like dried up fuel etc) but actually luck was playing in our favour, we reached the venue around 10.00 am and the venue sucked it was a horrible place to keep a gathering, it was a concert hall and the show started with the lights on! At least in SG hall it was dark and we could scream out like me and asif did in teacher's day. The first performance was given by prasad who used to look like a typical kid from the streets of bihar and nobody takes him seriously on a medival hindi song and no surprises here as usual nobody took him seriously and made fun of him by keeping an alias of his name as "krissh"

Time was running really slow I was beginning to feel restless as from the moment I set my foot in that amazing hall I was searching for one person and that person was amrita after an hour of daunting performance which was to horrible to see I finally saw her, she was as beautiful as she ever was she was wearing a black long tops which was almost like an anarkali type and it revealed her assets shape perfectly it was not cupped. "mostly she didn't wear her bra." I thought to myself and a black pencil fit jeans which made me fall in love with her big round ass. she finally noticed me staring at her beauty and gave me a chicky smile, one thing I love about her smile is that when she smiles it appears as though her eyes smile for her and I managed to regain hold of my senses and smiled back and waved at her. while all this was going on asif was chatting with isha and he was planning to go out with her after the useless programmes got over, she responded immediately and told asif that she was heading to the glass house which was the exact opposite building. the program ended within a short time but it seemed like an eternity when mrs. suresh gave a long speech on how the college was built ect.. the only enjoyable part of the program was a dance by a good looking first year girl on a popular item number "kamali kamali" and the food was just not eatable for me I really don't dig into sambar rice and papad in a gathering.

We finally managed to get out of the hall and after half an hour of being on the side of the road. asif dragged me and nashi into the glass house, as soon as we entered the glass house, which was an old building made of of iron and not even a single glass on the building. asif called isha and told her about his plans on meeting her alone, isha was a bit reluctant to go alone with asif and she said that seema should tag along to which asif agreed with a bit of disappointment and later seema said that she will hangout only if nashi tagged along.. I thought I'll go home and that asif and nashi will have fun. but nashi "forced" me to come along and so did isha!! after the plans where decided we started to roam around the park where we saw a few of our classmates including abhishek and prasad. after seeing us abhi tried to hide his new lumia 620, mostly because he kept some really private text between him and 3D which probably half of the college knew already and prasad came up to asif and took rather snatched his head phone after 20 mins of having some lays and soft drink we left the nerds to do their job and we continued near the aquarium which had small golden fishes hiding behind a sunken ship. Much like our life's, we hide behind the joy in life. And try to forget about the sufferings. we saw some hot 1st year girls. Me and asif where targeting a incredibly hot girl who used to chat a lot with chiru bhai, while nashi was on phone with seema and making plans. we tried for a long time to talk to her and yeah obviously we followed her gang and I bet they noticed it.

"bro you think they noticed us"?? asif asked me still checking out the girl.

"let's see we have been following them around for a long time and they are roaming around in circles and we are still following them!! so yes bro I think they know." I told him and continued to check out the same girl.

"trust me bro girls always know when you are behind them." asif said with yeah 'I am a pro' look.

"soo lemme guess since we are following a gang of girls they won't be sure which one we are checking out and each one of them will be thinking that they are better looking then other so they won't know who we are targeting??" I said with a smirk on my face.

"yeah bro!! there is a reason why you are my best buddy, you think like me." asif said and gave a knuckle's up.

After about spending two hours in the glasshouse isha called us up and told us to come to the parking lot and after some time we where set to go to K.F.C in urban oasis mall. Me and asif where on his bike, nashi riding his moppet alone, isha and seema on isha's scooty, after dodging a few traffic police and red signals we reached urban oasis, after reaching there we discovered a huge truth. half of my college was there. "what the fuck is going on??" I thought to myself

After we found a nice cozy place to sit. nashi came up with an ingenious idea that first we three guys will place our orders then the two madam's. this was because we didn't want to pay for them. after we placed our orders, isha and seema where nervous to place it as they never did it before at least that's what they told me after which I went to stand in the huge rows in front of the counters and nashi gave me his cash as I was a bit low on bucks at that time I had lost around 3k is in a street race which I thought I could win.. I ordered 2 chicken shots. When I was back at the place where my buddies were. those two chicks disappeared. guess what?? They brought all of us some yummy chicken burgers between the time when isha bought us the burgers nashi said "bey asif!! Are you going to propose isha now??

"mostly abhi kartha (well do it now)" asif replied.

"broo if you told it to me earlier I would have brought my guitar and played a romantic number for you and isha" I commented nashi and I where laughing, but asif had that serious look on his face that he was goin to do it.

"broo if you don't propose her then we will say that you love her!!" nashi said and to which I gave a serious affirmative nod.

Now isha and seema had been back, our convo started with the usual questions such as "did you like the show etc and everyone agreed that it sucked and after discussing about some lame topics asif was about to say something when kiran did the unexpected "asif ko thujhse pyar hogaya hai" (asif is in love with you) pointed kiran said rather screamed in a confession tone and was pointing towards isha.. "actually wo thujhe ab propose karnai wala tha" (he was going to propose you now" I said looking towards the shocked eyes of asif which clearly expressed (the fuck just happened feeling) which is seen in most teens eyes when there crush is flirting with someone else in front of there eyes. isha appeared to be in shock but asked "asif such mai kya??(really asif)" she wanted asif to say yes and grab her smooch here then and there, I guess you could see it in her eyes, as folks say 'we can make out if a person is in love with another person just by the way they stare at them.'

But asif said that he was just joking and me and nashi took it seriously, one could clearly see the disappointment on his face and his fake smile. and tugged my leg under the round K.F.C table "don't kick me bro say your true feelings now!! I shouted "sorry it was leg uh??" asif questioned me trying not to make things obvious. "then did you think it was isha's leg or what??" seema commented with a huge grin on her face, me and nashi where trying to control our laughter but as seema said those words and asif's face shrunk we could not control it anymore "asif is like my brother okay??!!!" isha said and looked at every one hoping we would stop laughing her cute brownish face had literally become pinky purple in A. shyness B. awkwardness. But after seeing our brother's face after isha said those exact words and asif's eyes where almost filled in tears me and nashi laughed uncontrollably!!! I have to admit it. the moment you see your best friend's crush call him as her brother and seeing your buddies helpless shocked face you will always ended laughing in an insane manner no matter how bad the situation may be.

"You are in a relationship with Vikram shetty right??" Nashi asked Isha pointing his sharp noise at her in a questioning manner. Isha was surprised by it, Seema was taken aback, I was quite shocked and Asif lets just say he was devastated, I am sorry but there was no kind way of saying that. "Yes I am!!" Isha was blushing, "But how do you know??" "I have my sources" Nashi said, "How many months rather...... How many years have you guys been in a relationship??" Asif asked with his sad and sunken eyes and his fake smile still on his shrunken face. "Not even a week yet!!"Nashi replied with a rather a type of grin that is see on the villain's face right before climax in the bollywood movies. And chewed on his chicken burger. Now I was totally dumbstruck. Nashi knew it all along and still played along with us and set up

Asif for a humongous disappointment!! "Nashi you sick slick" I thought to myself.

After some fun chatting (only for me and nashi it was fun, if you ask my buddy he will probably say that it was horrific) it was time to head home. While going home, isha wanted to ride nashi's moppet. but asif made me get down from his bike. "bhosdi kai haram chutiya gadi sai utar. (get the fuck off my bike.)" where his exact words and told isha to sit behind him. "I want to ride his bike." isha said with her incredibly cute childish voice. "you can drive it whenever you want!! Its like my bike itself." asif argued amd finally I was driving nashi's moppet alone, nashi and seema where on isha's scooty and asif and isha where on asif's bike. isha and asif spoke their mind out during the travel as I was constantly seeing them in my side mirrors. And as any guy would do we three slowed our speeds, alooooooot so we would chat a little longer with the galz, near the junction, we exchanged back to our proper vehicles and they went their way and we went straight.

Virat and chiru's double date with the devil

As if told to every V.N.C student even virat and chiru bhai along with their date's anitha and anamika where on gokul road itself and that to near the oasis mall junction. Virat and anitha where in a relationship from a long time and where chatting with their hands held together. Whereas, chiru bhai and anamika where the naughty new born type and where playing and groping each other on the same deserted street. Even though not many people use that wide stretch of road because many still do think that its under construction and is not yet officially opened, only very few people use that road from the area where my college is located to the airport during the peak hours of traffic. but as though the devil himself had blessed all the four of them, our princi was taking the exact same route and did manage to see the whole thing. but didn't react much. even virat the most paranoid person I've met till now. didn't care about the party crasher and resumed their work, it's the kind of work every teen, young adults and most of the middle aged people enjoy.

"virat and chiranjeev to the principal chamber now." announced the big black speakers located on each four corners of the library. "bro virat and chiru are fucked man!!" asif remarked and continued with solving some differential equations. "yes but not as much as you got fucked by isha in KFC yesterday." bharat said and we burst out laughing. "thiru you son of a bitch you can't keep your mouth shut or what?" asif asked me with a certainty that I spread the sensational, hot news to everyone. "I didn't even tell bharat that we went to KFC bro." I said trying to claim my innocence. "I don't need to hear from the people closest to you to get information about anything, I have my sources." Bharat was all boastful when he said it. I have to agree though he does get the news quicker than anyone else does, actually he was the one that told us about virat and chiru getting caught by our princi in their private moment. After about an hour and half later chiru entered the library a.k.a solitary confinement by barging in and slamming the door shut any one could make out that he was pissed, his white skin that reminded me of a popular WWE wrestler 'sheamus' had turned red partially because of his punishment in the princi's chamber and partially because of his anger.

"see brother's only guys get screwed very much in these matters nobody especially the lectures will even question the girls." bharat said in a lecturing tone. "and why is that?? Care to elaborate??" asif said in a taunting way. "I will pay attention to the guru!" he said "sex guru???!!" I said. And we could hear our laughs echo through the library. "I am not going to teach you 'kamasutra' as I know that you will be watching those videos with at most care and concentration. let me explain it anyway nobody will question the girls if they get caught in such matters in our country because the girl's honour is at stake." he said with his eyes bulging out and slowly expanding each and every word in his sentence.

Just Then, one of our college peons entered the library with a white sheet with a few roll numbers written on it. me and asif where panicking as we thought it was that time of the week where our princi goes through our daily exam results and one fine day call's us to his chamber and screws us all up badly. And after the harsh session we will be under the scanner for about three days, I really mean that. we had camera's located in both the side's of the room, on all four sides and we will be watched most of the time for those three days. The feeling in those three days is hard to explain and to understand. unless you are a girl, it was like those three tough days of the month. "what the fuck bro?? they just called us three days back!! Again we should go and get our ass's fucked or what??" asif exclaimed in a disappointed manner. "bro if they call out my number say that I am absent, I will escape and go house." bharat told me and asif in his paranoid look which we got to see quite frequently. "roll numbers 11 and 034 to the principle chamber." said the peon to our surprise both anita and anamika got up and the peon escorted the ladies to the chambers "they are hell bound!" I thought to myself. "bro did you see the guy who explained about girl's honour and said they won't get screwed?? For me it looks like everyone is gonna get it equally." I said as the grin on my face grew wider, looking at bharat "yeah yeahhhh yeaahh!! Whatever dude but it happens in most of the cases." bharat made a weak protest.

Shortly after meeting anamika and anita a phone call had gone to the couple's parents and they where informed to meet our princi by noon of the next day.

The date of 21st December, the Christmas spirit was setting in and we where waiting for the much anticipated break of two days the day went by pretty much normally and in the noon during our lunch break we saw virat standing beside his dad with head low. "thaaad" the loud sound of the slap on virat's face echoed threw the spacious reception hall "what the fuck??? In front of everybody damn in front of first years that got to leave a mental scar." asif said in a pitiful tone of voice. "I bet the scar is not going to be as prominent as the mark of his dad's right hand on his cheek." I said just then bharat had had come down from the last floor also know as the floor of solitary confinement and said "this place suckz man!! That old cunning bastard. We know that virat studies well but that fucker princi showed virat's dad only the marks in which he failed, he didn't even mention that virat is the physics topper to his dad and added more spice to that road incident…." "what the??? Did virat just get slapped by his dad in front of everyone? He continued "hey fucker how do you get these news man??? And what is more annoying is that everything you say is legitimate." "I have my sources" bharat said with a cunning smile with his eyes glowing. "let me find your sources!! I'll probably kill them. can't they fucking mind their own business??" asif assured bharat, you could clearly sense the seriousness in his voice when he said the sentence "can't they mind their own business."

The next day virat was early to school, he was in a bad state. his eyes where swollen and bloodshot anyone could make out his prominent dark circles around his eyes from a mile away. He kept things pretty much to himself the whole day and secluded himself from other, his dad had confiscated his mobile, and his brand new pulsar 200 ns bike. On the other hand, chiru bhai was pissed off at everything and anything that crossed his way. "shhhissh!! he is screaming like a hurt gorilla!!" asif commented covering his hears with his hands "he Is built like a gorilla and he is also hurt, so it makes sense that he is screaming like one." bharat added trying to figure out on how to solve his statistic sum, his buddy swastik who used to help him out in stat was absent that day. "I got to get me some ear plugs. one reason is that I don't want the gorilla to scream my head off and the other reason is the obvious one I don't wanna hear lame jokes of the great bharat." I said while facebook'ing, the trend was that whenever bharat had statistics exam me and asif used to have biology exam on the same day. I always considered myself to be good at biology, so I preferred to annoy bharat during those days of exam. Chiru bhai had got to know that virat's bike had been confiscated and offered him a ride home, to which virat clearly declined saying the idea was a one way ticket to hell but he did reluctantly agree after some strong persuasion's by chiru who said that he wanted to resolve the dispute with virat's dad. I was just about to leave when chiru needlessly tagged me along and trust me when I say this he doesn't take no for an answer, he is like a cement wall with thorns. all the reluctance you have will get shredded by his persuasion and you will end with him even if you don't like it. "oooh damn it!! It's so not going to end well!!!" I thought to myself as we begin our voyage towards virat's home which was located in the other side of the city.

"hey who are you man? And how dare you come inside my house" virat's dad growled at chiru and was boiled up as a steam engine, his dad was in no mood to listen rather he didn't feel the need to listen to chiru, after all he was the only cunning, game playing, sick son of a bitch who was going to spoil his son's life right??. It was a really great deed that I didn't step inside and was on call with bharat while the drama unfolded in front of me. "bro abandon ship?? are you gonna get outta there??" bharat asked with excitement, almost begging for me to stay. why wouldn't he be so excited the next big sensational breaking news was taking place and I was the one reporting it to him. "no!! Not yet man lets see what happens." I replied him. I could hear chiru apologizing to him and said that he wanted to explain his part of the story "thaad!!" virat's dad sent another hot blow to the already grief stricken face of virat. virat kept his head down in utter dismay "uncle slap me if you want directly!! But I will not go from here until you hear me out." chiru told him with defiance. "whatever our princi said was not true uncle. virat studies well." "then how did he fail in all the three tests?? By mixing with you?" virat's dad asked him arrogantly "only three tests??? Uncle we would written more than a hundred tests. we write a test almost on daily basis. see this is what I wanted to tell you uncle, princi just showed you the marks in which virat failed but he didn't tell you that your son is the class topper in physics!!" virat's dad was silent, I took it as a sign of victory and thought things will get back to normal soon. "you have no respect towards your teachers also!! How low can you get?? fall on suresh sir's and principal's feet and beg them to forgive you otherwise you will never succeed in life. and don't tell me on how to raise my son I know that whatever your teachers are doing is my son's bright future." virat's dad said and pushed virat by his shoulder as if ordering him to go inside, like a puppy being forced to go inside its cannal. but virat didn't budge. "papa even after knowing all these you think they are doing it for my benefit?? you don't see that they are manuplating you?" virat stared dead straight into his dad's eyes. "go inside or else I'll kill you." his dad pushed him with his both the hands. "sir please don't do these things I will…." Before chiru could complete his sentence "you!!! You are the reason why my son has become like this!! He never disobeys me!! Now see he isn't following my command." virat's dad grunted at chiru and was about to slap virat again. "obey??, command?? Disobey??" virat mumbled these words as he kept his head down and sobbing, he didn't cry even when he was manhandled moments ago "obey you papa?? Command me?? disobeying you papa??" he said again this time his mumbles turned into screams. "I respected you papa" he stressed on the word 'pected' I loved you, you where my hero but now!?? Now I see the whole thing .." "see what beta (son)?? I really do love you. I want a bright future for you that's all." his dad said keeping his hand on virat's cheek. "thank god it isn't another slap." I said bharat as I was giving him the live feed. "just!! Just stoooop!! You understand responsibilities but you don't even know what is love… all those years I took your crap was because I loved you!! But now that I should obey you! And listen to your commands (he kept hands on his head and tried to pull off his hairs) I'll ensure that my future doesn't involve you anywhere in it, thanks a loot papa now I understand what I mean to you. I die every day in that hell and you say they are good people wanting a bright future for me?? You tell my friend to fall at our princi's feet, the same person who abuses us daily?? Thanks papa thanks a lot." virat said these words in such a way that a by stander will think that he is insane. "beta I just.." "just leave me alone. I am not your puppy any more." virat said and got out of his dad's grip and rushed into his room and bolted it from within, I still remember that pale expression on uncle's face it said they chiru was only responsible for what had happened minutes ago. "look sir! I know you will blame me for this and you may even complain about it. but the reason why I came here was to solve the problem. sir just believe your son sir. he is your son, your blood." chiru said and jogged out onto his bike "such a filmsy dialogue by chiru!!" bharat said on the other end of the line.

"bro why are our parent's like this man??" virat asked as he was puffing in his king's cigar, it had been two days since the incident took place and virat's dad further complained about chiru to the princi and told him everything that happened that day and told our princi to take care of virat by joining his hands together, in india we join our hands in our famous Namaste position to either welcome our guests or plead anything to others, it's the final step of pleading before falling at others feet and begging them for apology. "see prinici's care for me." virat said and showed his knuckles which appeared to be fractured, as there no flow of blood in that region and the whole region had turned purple. "now that's a bright future. And welcome to the canning club broo!!" I said and gave him a knuckles up. "the way they fucked both of us was tremendous bhai (bro)." chiru said sipping his beer "well you both got gang raped to be precise and yeah in front of everyone!" I said and sipped my glass of magnum platinum beer. "well at least we have this K.M.C ground to come and cool off whenever we get fucked up!!" virat said releasing his long puff of smoke. "well cheer's to that and also guys it's the last day of college before Christmas." I said and raised my glass up. "yeah right we are just getting two days off, what is the big deal in that and I am sure someone or the other will keep an exam the day school re-open's" chiru said "well that's why I said last day of school before Christmas, not last day of school before winter break! Note the difference." I said with a smirk on my face "cheers!!" chiru said and slammed his bottle to mine which nearly knocked my bottle off my hand "careful man 125rs a bottle." I said "and what happened to anamika and anita??" I asked virat who finished smoking his second packet of the day. "princi didn't say anything much to their parents except what we where doing on the road that day, they just lost there phone privilege's that's all." virat said "that's because both of them brought their sister's, they didn't get a strict notice that they should only bring their father to meet the princi it seems." chiru said lighting his first cigar of the day. "but the way you said those words man!! straight from your heart. Seriously our dad's are our first hero, we look up to them for everything. our parents say that we change as we grow old but they don't realize that they have a fare share in that as well. I mean we are not throwing a fit because we didn't get a new play station or a brand new bike, we are trying hard for them to listen to the torture we go through almost every alternative day." I said as I finished half of my bottle "I could not agree with you more!! here want a smoke??" chiru offered me a menthol cigar. "no bro I don't smoke I have asthma remember?" I said and continued to sip on my drink. "hey we are eighteen bro!! it's our fault only.. anything bad happens to us, we are solely responsible and if we do anything good that's because of our parents effort." virat said and we all where smiling. "paying fee to the tuitions, schools and all I agree its their soul effort it's their hard earned money. But throwing us in a fucking jail and not hearing a word we say on the basis that we are eighteen and further up give info to the people that are torturing us daily!!! and telling them that we say bad things about them to others. so that we get tortured some more the very next day when they find out is just……….. epic!! I salute the mentality of our parents" chiru said and stood up on a near by chair and saluted into the thin air, the air was chilly and there where light evening drizzles and thunders which are not uncommon during the monsoon in india, just added flavor to the topic we where discussing about.. "you forgot bro!! Our parents tell our torturers to take care of us also!!" I said and showed them the bruises on my knuckles, we burst out laughing. "dude I could see that shekar and princi torture you, haven't you thought of killing them??" virat asked me keenly. "I have thought about it. But they are not worth the effort, besides killing them is not a big thing." I continued to drink my glass of beer. "not a big thing?? Because you are what? World's most feared underworld don???" chiru bhai said and kicked me from behind. "no it is because I am not yet eighteen unlike you both, I am still a juvi bro. that means even if I kill them I will get three years tops, in a correctional home. It is not like the US, where you can be tried as a juvi or an adult.

In our country we are tried as juvi itself. Besides our body shows signs of getting physically abused, so for example if I kill shekar with a lets say a botanical needle, which every bio student will have in the dissection kit. If I just jab the needle once in his carotid artery he will die, but it will look pre meditated. So when he hits me madly again, all I have to do is scream out loud and start stabbing him madly with the needle. it will make the killer strike look like an accident. And I also have my insanity plea, so it is no problem doing it." I said and watched them look at me, with their eyes popping out. "dude. I didn't think that you…. I mean you!! Can think like this." Chiru bhai told me in astonishment. "then why not just do it?" virat asked me seriously. "because if I do it, then I won't have a life. People will think I am insane, they will be scared to get near me. And suddenly you will be the bad guy. And all these days of torture will go for a waste. I want some fruit for my struggle bro." I told him, making sure he understands the consequences. "understood, don't worry I won't kill anybody." Virat told us with a smile, that appeared to fake. "so what are you going to do man?? Start hating your dad, inherit all his property and throw your parents in an old age home?" this time I was the curious one. "no! I love my dad. And even though I fought with him, I am still living in his house. And I don't need his properties man. I am the one living in his house. Not the other way around." This was the first mature answer I got from virat in a long time. "what about your future plans then??" chiru asked him. "I will prepare for NDA(national defense academy) and join the army." Virat said and his natural smile started to appear. "what about you man?? Future plans?" virat asked me keenly. "me……assuming I walk out of here, which is unlikely…" "everyone chance's is unlikely here. Just cut the crap and say." Chiru asked me impatiently. "I am a screw up on land, so mostly I will be a seafarer, mostly a marine engineer or an oil rigger." "that is so obvious, bad childhood, over powerful and abusive dad, no shelter to be with anyone. We have to join the army, or in your case the merchant navy." Virat said and finished his third packet of the day. "it is getting late bhai!! I will leave now and thanks for the beer thiru!" chiru said as he was about to leave. "that's no problem bro, besides when a bunch of hurt guy's sit around for a chat. A beer in each one's hand is a must!" I said and got up to leave. "well in my case, I'll just settle with cigar's." virat said finishing his last smoke of the day and getting ready to leave "chiru!!" I screamed he had gone done about 50 steps and was near his bike "why don't you drop virat home??" I said and chiru replied me by swinging his middle finger. "ooh!! That finger give's a direct answer to most of the questions." I told virat and left him near the bus stop and made my way home.

Welcome 2014

Bro!! you, me and Nashi will party like crazy man!!" Asif told us with full of excitement.. "What about 58??"I asked Asif and was staring at Amrita who was a surprise guest to the library for the day, she had come there to study by choice whereas we ......Is just another story. "I asked him! his parents won't allow it seems.." "well its 30th now lot can happen in two days" I said trying to lift up our spirits "Are you kidding?? Seriously??? Our parents??" Nashi commented with a smirk on his face. The whole day passed by, with our planning of the party, Bharat was a bit dull and was not interested in our whole discussion. "Hey fucker!! Don't get so upset and all I will come and convince your parents and assure your parents that we won't go to goa, or visit a strip club" Asif screamed from the corner of his seat. "I'll try to come dude.. But I don't think that I will make it." Bharat told us, with his dull voice. I saw that Amrita had got up from her seat and was walking towards the door, her hips where moving side to side and she was driving me crazy. I just had to get up and speak to her. "Hii!! Amrita!!" I said trying to keep a descent smile, I didn't want her to think that I was some weird ass stalker "Hi.. how is the planning going on??" she asked me with her beautiful smile and her eyes glowing. "Damn she knows that we are organizing a party"... Well it's hard for someone to not over hear our conversation as we were talking about it the whole day. "Yes we are planning a little something." I was still smiling at her. "Ask her out to the party!! Ask her out to the party!! Fucker just ask her out to the party." I was talking to myself, there was an internal debate taking place inside me "So ..... What brings you up here to the solitary confinement section of the prison???" I asked her cursing myself for not asking her out. "Down stairs They are taking some CET(common entrance test) classes and it's really boring. So I thought that I will do some self-study in the library." she replied, her pink lips where widened, her smile was like spotting an oasis in the dry hot dessert, the way she tossed the few strands of her hair which was only curly at its ends and which covered her face at times was magical. The way she adjusted it back to its rightful place which in turn exposed her bright smiling face full of joy was something angelic to me. "ooh that is cool!! Feels good to talk to you after so many days." I told her, trying not to expose my awestruck side to her. "Well now only I got to know that you still remember me. You come into the class at times, but you just irritate Abhishek and go off, you don't even tell me a 'HI' or 'bye'." Amrita said smiling, not with her cherry like lips but with her eyes. "Oooh that is quite complicated! Anyways plans for new year's eve?? and may I have your....." Just before I could ask her number I was interrupted by Shekar sir who commanded me to go back to the library and resume the studying. "Man what the fuck??? This is unreal!! This type of shit doesn't even happen in movies these days!!! Why now????"I was blabbering things to myself, I tried to turn back and look at her but Shekar sir was right behind me and was pushing me forward every time I slowed down. Before I entered into the library I got a glimpse of her looking straight at me, I looked at her with dismay and waved at her "bye..." she said and waved me back with a smile which seemed a little too artificial.. "How on earth will a girl date you if she see's you get manhandled in front of her??" I was cursing myself and made a mental note of breaking Shekar's right hand after I got my results.

31st December 2013, nashi backed out of the party which we had painstakingly had planed and he said that he cannot come as his sister will be alone in his home so his parents didn't allow him "that's a lame excuse right??" I said looking at asif who was steaming in anger "he is lying just for the record I'll say it again that son of a bitch is lying" asif said with disappointment and finally by the end of the day we decided that me, asif and few of his friend will party.

"bro I can't come!! My dad is screaming at me." asif said on phone "ok!! No probie I'll party with the two sexy chicks next door like I did last year" I replied and said "beta I am the baap of the game (son I invented that mind game) to myself "fine bro! enjoy the party and so sorry that I wouldn't make it." and the call got disconnected, for the starting five minutes I didn't react but then I thought to myself. "what will happen if asif back's out as well?? I can't stay home on new year's eve." "hey fucker!! Where are you??" I texted him and there was no reply, this was the time when I thought the whole thing is going to get fucked up and checked on the girls they had already left to a premium party in gateway taj. I cursed myself for not keeping a back up party where I could just join on, I was dumbstruck I mean I was

dressed up packed up my towels, tooth brush and a my
school uniform and I was actually ready for a sleep over.
I was pissed off and removed my shirt and was untied my
shoelaces when suddenly I got a call from asif. "yeah say!
I grunted at him, thinking that it will those apologizing
calls for formalities "I am sorry for the confusion and I also
know that your pissed as anyone can sense that within a
one block radius from you and yeah dress back up. I'll be
in front of your house in five minutes." "dude I am glad
that you are coming man. I didn't want 2k14 ti start with
a disappointment" after fifteen minutes asif had arrived in
front of my house and I bid my parents goodbye and began
heading to the party which we had been planning since
two days and it almost collapsed. on the way we dropped
by nashi's house to confirm that he was out "nashi come
down broo we are standing in front if your house." I said
and waited eagerly for the reply "han!! I am not home man,
iam with my school friends" nashi said in a nervous way "for
the record we knew that you lied." I said and asif snatched
away my phone "abbey saale maderchod, harami kutte essa
double game kyun kheltha bey (why the fuck do you play
double games man??) "well dude at least lets hit the bar now
before it gets too crowded" I said trying to cheer him up,
well he did fight in his house just to come for the little party
which we organized.

At the bar the scene was chaotic, it was like being caught in
middle of a stampede. I felt that every guy who hit puberty
in hubli was in that bar and people seemed to but gallons
of alcohol. after waiting for nearly twenty minutes in the
overcrowded bar we finally managed to get some whiskey

and a magnum platinum 750ml, which usually costs about 125rs was up to 150rs for that particular day. after getting our hands on the beauty we proceeded out with great caution of not getting caught with it by our family, neighbours, self righteous teetotaller classmates whose PG rooms happened to be near that bar, we didn't want them to notice us because if one of them gets to know the matter will reach the hears of my princi and we will be forced to get a memorable gift for the new year by him and that we preferred not to. we headed to asif's tuition friends PG room, the room was quite spacious and had huge grilled windows which provided the constant supply of cool air in the room, It was like a typical guys room with clothes where kept all around the place and in another corner a huge pile of book was kept. there was a list of math formulae's sheet which was stuck on the front door, I was expecting a bunch of posters of nude girls which was not there. "damn if they are too descent I'll feel a bit guilty drinking in front of them" I thought to myself. after my formal intro to shravan and manthesh we got into some random talks and after a while of chatting I was clear that asif didn't disappoint with the choice of our guest list except with nashi that is. "hey guys I brought a little gift here" I said and opened the bottles of whiskey and beer which was wrapped around in a black plastic cover "super boss!! I thought you will not drink and all so we have to be descent" shravan said opening the bottle of beer "brother I'll never forget you in my life. you are the first one that said I don't look like I drink and I am very descent" "why boss?? You drink a lot?? Well its not uncommon for a student of V.N.C to get addicted to drinking!! I heard you people get hit by a wooden duster and all?? Is that true?" shravan asked has he had a sip of beer. "arrey bhai just don't remind me why I drink now yeah?? Without this baby I can't even sleep in the night." I said and had my sip of whiskey with coke. we got a call from nashi around 10.30 and he tried to explain himself to us, to which asif remained indifferent and nashi told us to come near KA 25 which is a popular café and a place well reputed for the hot premium parties they threw. As my parents didn't allow me to take my bike out for the night and there were four of us left with one bike, we decided to walk till reliance digital a supermarket not so far from the PG room. "you could have brought your bike no?? we heard that you are a badass racer" monty said while walking towards the place "well monty I am surprised that my parents allowed me to come out for a new year celebration!! So I don't press my luck much." I said "and thanks man!! I feel good when somebody calls me a badass racer" "you take pride in it??" asif said while dragging his bike beside him "well not as much as you do.. I might be quicker than him on wheels guys but he is the master of controlling the ride." I announced to everybody "asif that's shruti's house right?" shravan taunted asif, shruti was the girl who was dating asif during the time, she had quite the attitude has she knew that she was beautiful and guys tried their luck with her. She was the drama queen character types. "yeah I know that bro!! I have been in there quite frequently you know." asif taunted him back. Later I did come to that shravan had I crush on shruti but before he could make a single move she ended up dating asif.

"the biggest fucker of all time as just arrived!!! Ladies and gentlemen I present to you naaaaashi!!" asif said and was expecting an equally taunting reply from nashi. "sorry idiot. I'll explain it to you later!! Just hop on quick." he said as though he was in some sort of a hurry. Me and asif where on one bike and shravan, monty and nashi where on the other. Soon we reached near KA 25 we ordered some cakes and snacks there. "every girl in there are just red hot." monty said checking out a girl wearing a backless party ware. "and every girl in there is with their bf and the bouncers don't look friendly." I said pointing out towards a bouncer In the entrance he appeared to be around 6.5ft tall and weigh about 250 pounds and fully buffed up. "no problem bro! I think that girl is happy dancing with her bf." Finally we reached the place where the party was going on, It was on the terrace of sachin's house. sachin was nashi's buddy since high school and the fact that he lived with his brother who apparently went out to party with his friends made his place the right venue. we had the whole house to ourselves, there where about twenty five people there and after having chatted with them and slowly eased ourselves in. we started getting into the groove of things and we certainly began to enjoy ourselves. On top of the terrace there where some big speakers and some light effects system installed and a mini disco ball which also added to the lighting effect and gave out some time based flashes. There was some loud pitbull and Enrique iglesias mix that was being played and the woofers certainly did make us enjoy the numbers more.. "should we just sit around here? Or lets play a game of truth and dare??" pavan, my pu college mate said as he got up and told us to form a circle. "why the same old game??" nashi protested, but we ended up playing it as there are not many games to play that is interesting enough with such crowd and everyone did want to talk to the four girls who had come to the celebration and starting the chat by asking some questions while playing a game was a good way to start. We did have a great time playing the game of truth and dare, since no one was interested in doing the dare we played only the truth part of the game. there was all sorts of questions asked. Questions about who our crushes where? How many times did we propose?? Some even asked who our favourite pornstar was and so on.

"hi bro!! guess what my parents finally allowed me to go out!" bharat said with excitement, I could barely hear him though "that is great!! Can you come near KA 25 I'll pick you up there??" "what?? I can't hear you clearly man" "I WILL PICK YOU UP NEAR KA 25!!" I screamed over the phone "no!! I am with my school friends now!! You enjoy man!! Don't drink too much I'll see you tomorrow" bharat said and he hung up. there was just 15 minutes left for 2k14 to arrive, it was the year that I had been waiting for two years. this was the year in which I can go back home again. This was the year my jail sentencing ends. it started to strike me that I will be hanging around with asif and bharat for just another three months and then our chances of meeting each other will be less. "damn I can't see amrita after these three months!!" I thought to myself but I was sure glad that my days in hubli was coming towards the finish line. Asif and nashi were getting around fine now as me and asif insulted him and his crush badly during the game of truths, so there was no hard feelings to anyone and we were even. Around 11.55 some people brought the cakes and the snacks up and had the foam canister and ready. in a few watches it was already 12.00 am and we could hear the fireworks going off but sachin was sure that it was 11.59 and not yet 12.00, so we formed a circle and kept really quite till the countdown began "10,9,8,7!!,6!!,5!!,4!!,333333, 222222!!!, 1!!!!!!! Happy new yearrrrrr!!!!!!" we all shouted and started jumping around in the circle, the ending five numbers of the countdown always gave me the goosebumps. we started jumping around in the circle and started making around 10 rounds, we were screaming our heads off!! The fireworks started to go out in full swing. And the next moment I remember is catching my spectacles in my hand and someone was smashing my face with the chocolate cake and there was white foam all over my head. We were hugging and wishing everybody present there including the girls who were silent most of the time. "bing!!!bing!! bing!!bing!!" the texts and calls started to pour in like meteorites. And finally after another two joy rounds in the 25 men (four girls also) and clicking a lot of photos we decided to head home has all of us had coll the next day. my dad started calling me and told me to get back home "so much for the sleepover plan" I thought. I informed this to my friends who let me go after I explained the whole thing to them in detail, nashi agreed to come till the PG room and drop me back home and asif would be with his buddies for the sleepover. On the way to the PG we saw three people selling stuff mostly coke and asked us if we wanted any?? We didn't slow our bikes a bit because even if they are not drug dealers they could be robbers.

Back in the room I quickly finished my whiskey and was about to hit on some beer, but as I was getting repeated calls from my dad I could just complete half of the bottle "happy new year guys!! Take this as a present" I said and gave the bottle to shravan and after waving goodbye to my mates, I sat behind nashi as I really wasn't in a condition to drive it took us about 15 mins for us to reach my house from the PG room. "idiot!! Go silently and sleep and don't fall while climbing the stares and try not to puke in front of your house!!" nashi said with an evil smile. "I won't my capacity is a lot!! Happy new year bhai!! Drive safe". I knocked on the door and waited for my dad to open it "happy new year" he said with his hand extended out to me "happy new year daddy." I said and shook his hand, and hit the bed immediately. I was a bit unstable. "that happens when you drink whiskey and beer fast." I thought to myself. My head was spinning "maybe I should've gone for that cool party which was going on in an open ground with awesome music and disco lights, it was certainly a nice view to see before coming home." I slowly dozed off to sleep which was one of the best sleep I had in a while.

New day of the new beginning

"Wake up!! Its already 6.50 and happy new year" my sister said over the other end of the phone. "hmmm I got up!! And happy new year." I said with my sleepy voice, my head was hurting and my eyes appeared small and bloodshot. this new year's eve was was way cooler than the previous one where I partied with two of my sexy neighbours, but this one was awesome even if it didn't require two sexy sauji girls to party with. I reached my college around 7.30, I was having a bad hangover and I was still sleepy. even though I went to bed around 2.00am my school friends woke me up by 4.15am, that was the exact time was my one if the many calls that dawn.

"Yes! Waran when are you going to write the test?? Now or at 9.00??" Shekar sir a.k.a millimeter asked me with his cunning eyes "ooh fuck!! I have a test today?" I felt as if I was getting split into two "9.00 will be fine sir" I said with a respectful smile "okay" centimeter remarked and walked away with his 5.1 ft tall body and self proclaimed NSG commando brain, "he is not even fit to wipe the shoe of an NSG commando and he claims himself as commando trained. damn it I can't belive that I let him manhandle me in front of amrita." I said to Kiran. "may I come in sir??" asif asked with his voice barely audible and his eyes where bloodshot too. "its 8.30 now!! What where you doing last night?? By looking at your's and your friend's face itself I can make out what you people did" centi screamed from the other end of the library. "hey I know how you came to know that?" Kiran shouted and pretended that as if he was studying. After not saying another word for almost a minute, he continued "did you study for the test?? At least did you know that you have a test??" "yes sir!! I just need to brush up" said asif with 'I am so fucked up' reaction. "come on time from tomorrow." we finished writing our test within an hour and at 10.00 am we was bharat chatting along with his classmates, he looked more fresh then us. "drank too much last night??" swastik asked me, he also appeared to be hung "is it that obvious??" "yes bro. your eyes are shrunk and completely red" bharat said keeping a wide smile on his face.

The rest of the day was good, we greeted every teacher and friends.. "Happy new year!!" "Ooh hi! Happy new year to you also." Amrita told me with her smile, that smile there is something there in that smile. "Did you party yesterday??"I asked her "Yes!!but only with my family...... I am sure that you partied a lot. I can see it" she taunted me and her smile grew wider. "Well that's because I didn't sleep that well." I said and tried to look away from her eyes "Waran!! I saw your fb status which read "yo guys its time to welcome 2k14 with a magnum beer and whiskey. Daaamn no hot chicks around." she told me as her eyes began to shrink in her cheeks. "Ooh that one!! That's just....... uuuuhh ummmmm........ Yeah I did have some of it and plus it would've been great if you were there with me." I said trying hard to make a sensible sentence. "Says a guy who didn't even call to wish me!!" she said with her left eye brow raised.

"Yup. I didn't have your number. Sorry but can I have it now??" I asked her hoping that she will give it "no problems I was just joking.... And my number is 89**********" she said with her eyes that smile for her. "Okay. Will call you sometime!! Bye enjoy your day." "sure.. you too bye" she said and was about to leave. "And Amrita!!! not doing your self-study up in solitary confinement??"I asked her, a part of me already knew the answer "Aahaa.. After seeing what Shekar did to you na, I prefer not to come up now!! You take care okay?" I did not know what to take her care as, she was the only one that bothered to appreciate my presence. Whilst everybody thought I was a walking dead, breathing oxygen. I wanted to believe it was love, but it wasn't the time. When I could convince myself. "Ooh that's no probs, I'll give my appreciation to him later!! You too take care." "Bye!!" she said with her smile and went away into with her hips swaying side to side as she walked into the class.

"broo!! I got amrita's number" the excitement, in my voice, could be heard from a mile away. it's a big moment when your crush gives you his/her number. "32-28-34 is it??" bharat said with a smirk on his face. "son of a bitch!! She gave me her phone number asshole." I grunted "chill out dude. just kidding!! So you won't sleep properly tonight also uuh??" bharat said looking behind me. Princi, suresh and ram sir were making their way towards the library. "I don't care in which meaning you said that, but by the look of things I bet that's what is going happen" I commented back "now what are these assholes here for?? I jus got my knuckle canning last week!!" asif said in a panicking tone of voice. "I am sure they are not here to wish us new year" bharat said looking straight into princi's eyes "ookay!! Students this is the timetable for the first pre-board examinations which is going to be held from 11th of this month" our princi said displaying the white sheet to all of us "those who fail in all the subjects can have a look at bharat's back for the consequence and those who fail in one or two subjects can look at thiru's or asif's knuckle for the consequences." Princi said giving a wicked grin to me and caught my hand to display their art work on my knuckles. "sir show asif's hand also sir!!" suresh sir said and held his hand high. "sir they are both thick friends sir. Whatever they do they will do together, they even fail in one subject each to give each other company in the library sir." suresh said with a sentence that had a lot more meaning then he said. "I don't know about other things but we will burn you together for sure.." I thought to myself and forcefully freed my hand from princi's grip "and for the rest of the students who fail. your chance's of getting the hall ticket will be very thin, so study well and students happy new year." ram said with his pan stained mouth. Dude I think my hangover is gone now" I said nudging asif's shoulder "fucker now my head is spinning" asif said with a shocked expression "I am getting a strange hallow feeling in my stomach man" nashi said, now he was fully in his senses. He slept the whole day in the benches placed before the corridor. "so two years in hell is coming to a climax now!!" I said with a smirk on my face "yeah...it seems so!!" bharat said in a worried way

First taste of life

As the days passed like years the D-day had arrived, we had chemistry exam on the first day, we didn't get any study holidays or so. The chemistry paper went really well, it was given from the model papers, which the prisoners in solitary confinement wing studied the whole day. and after the exam got over we had regular classes. being in the library had its own privileges, we had more time to study for the upcoming exam, my physics paper went quite well, bio was awesome as usual and I was absolutely sure that I was going to flunk in math.

During the days between pre board results we did enjoy a lot. me, nashi, bharat, asif and shruti went to "nrupatungabeta" as to celebrate after the extreme week of exams. asif and shruti where riding together, I was alone, as only a few speed thrill seeking junkies can sit behind me while I drive and nashi and bharat were on nashi's bike it was 5.30 pm in the evening and we were nearing our destination, I was alone and enjoying the cloudy weather for the whole journey of 45 minutes. after reaching the place we all had a nice cup of elaichi tea in a shop on top of the hill, nrupathungabeta is a hill "beta" in kannada, a language spoken by the people in the southern part of india. asif and shruti quickly finished their cup of tea and disappeared somewhere. "he is going to make out with her" I said nashi and bharat with a smile "that's a guarantee bro, why do you think he brought her here?? This place is the lover's spot." told bharat as he lighted his black cigar "you have amrita's number right??" bharat asked releasing his long puff of black smoke "yup so??" "her house is near by idiot." he said with a higher frequency of voice "really how do you know?.... no don't answer that I know I know "you have your sources." I said by clicking my index and middle fingers of both my hands, he took another puff and said "then what are you waiting for??" "fucker seriously she lives near by??" I double checked and after getting his icy cold stare as a reply, I started to type my text "heyy!! Its thiru here hw was your exam?? and are you free now??" before I could lock my keypad and thank bharat for giving me the info, I got the reply quickly "hi!!it was nice..yes I am free now. y?" "oooh cool.. I am near your house J can we hangout now??" I texted her and was already sure that I'll get a negative reply, "there is no chance in hell that she will agree bro. maybe I'll change the topic??" I asked nashi who was sitting next to me "wait up!! you are paranoid man give her sometime." he replied in a cool way and sipped his tea. After five minutes I thought of texting her a sorry or talk about something else, I had began to type a sentence when I got a text from her again "okay sure. where are you??" "in nrupathungabeta..where is your house exactly?? "its about 5 minutes from there." "I'll pick you up in 10 minutes okie?" "sure J." "bro!! amrita is coming to meet me!!" I shouted rather hooted nashi and bharat instructed me to drive safely, as it was drizzling and not to do any road circus with a girl behind me. I reached her street in about 15 mins, where she was waiting for me. she was wearing a pink t-shirt and blue denim pencil fit jeans. "don't stare at her boobs. do not stare at her boobs." I told myself and said "hi!! Nice to see you again after a long time." with my helmet still on "hi thiru thanks for coming to pick me up" she said as she kept her hands over my shoulders for support and hoped on to my bike "daaamn thanks for coming?? a guy will kill if he has to, so that u can sit behind him." I said myself and started my bike.

After we reached the place I ordered two glasses of elaichi tea and meanwhile I noticed that nashi was talking on phone with someone with a fresh glass of tea and bharat started with his new cigar. me and amrita found a comfortable place to sit and we started to chat "you are looking beautiful as always." I remarked "oh thanks! Pink and blue are my favorite colour." she said with a sweet smile "so how was your day yr??" I asked her as I sipped my tea "it was boring, but now that you came and picked me up and brought me here. now its good" she said blowing her tea to make it a bit more cool, the way her lips formed an "O" shape while she blew it was mesmerizing to me, I wanted to kiss her then and there. "I am glad that you agreed to come. Otherwise, I would have been bored out of my mind." I said and moved closer to her "well I waited for 10 days to get your text." she said and adjusted her hair from covering her face, she appeared different to me that day. "holy shit!! she was waiting for me to text her!!" it was unbelievable I wasn't the most handsome of guys and she was the persona of the word beautiful "is this real??" I thought to myself, the wind started to pick up the pace and the drizzles began to get heavy. "this is the first time that I am coming here and it's an awesome view." I told her watching the scenic view from the top of the hill. "I've been here a lot of times but I haven't felt like this." she said and her fingers brushed my left fist. "then what is making it special?? Is it the awesome weather??" I asked "thiru!! you use the word 'awesome' a lot have you noticed??" she asked me with her cute larger than life smile "do I?? I don't think so??" I said nudging my shoulder against hers, it is my habit. "no it is not because of the weather." she said and turned her right shoulder towards me and looking straight into my eyes "then why?" "its because I just escaped from my house saying that I am going to my friends house to discuss the model papers, and sat back on a bike with a guy who didn't apply sudden breaks so that my body can brush against his and also he didn't propose, rather call or text immediately after getting my number." she said still looking into my eyes "what do you don't like about that guy??" I asked her looking straight into her beautiful eyes, which had some mascara on them. "and that guy rides his bike like crazy along with his crazy best friend and thinks of himself as a very big racer and I hate him because of that." she replied, we didn't take her eyes of each other "ouch that hurts!! then what do you like about him?" I smiled and I could feel her warm breath "I like it that he is sitting very close to me and looking at me straight in the eye." she said that and looked at my lips and then back into my eyes. "will you still like that guy if he kisses you now??" I asked her and moved my face closer to hers "how the hell did I just manage to say that?" I thought to myself, she didn't reply but rather kept staring into my eyes, my lips brushed her soft lips then she responded by taking my upper lip in hers, then I sucked her lower lip with mine and did the same with her upper lip and our tounge's played with each other's. we separated "that was my first kiss" I said while our forehead was in contact with each other "I could see that" she said with a naughty smile "was it even the correct way?? I could taste elaichi" I said rubbing my lips with my palm "you will learn it properly thiru." she said "me too I thought I'll taste vodka" she continued and caressed my hair with her palms.

After a while we had to leave because the rain was getting heavy. On the way back home Asif narrated us with excitement that he had kissed Shruti in a "tum hi ho" style, it was actually a song from a popular Bollywood movie, 'aashiqui 2' where the hero kisses the heroine while keeping his jacket over her head protecting her head from the rain, after she gets completely drenched. That way of kissing was getting popular back in the day. We all had a wide grin on our face, Bharat was waiting to hear me out. "Fucker we know... We were seeing the whole thing actually most of the people there would have seen it, I accelerated forward, all our bikes were in top gear. Although me and Amrita managed to find a comfortable place to sit, evidentally it was not secluded. "You in love with her man??? Don't fall in love with her and all. She is not the good girl types." Bharat screamed at me, I could barely hear him with the sound of the wind hitting my face. I lined my bikes speed along with Nashi's. "What the fuck did you just say about her??" I asked Bharat, what he said clearly pissed me off. "You have no fucking sense or what?? Are you mad?" Asif said as he too matched his bike speed with ours "You leave it man!! I just said for fun and you came to fight with me only!! After a girl comes friends disappear or what??" Bharat said trying to convince that he didn't mean it. "Hey.. I didn't want a fight with you and all man. I just didn't want you to make fun of her." I told him and we raced away to our house we were all drenched and I started preparing for my Physics test.

It was January 18th, I heard the voice of my sister waking me up but to my surprise it wasn't over phone she was standing in front of me. she had come over to my place, along with my brother in law. To celebrate "sankrathi", which is a harvest festival but generally specifies the celebration to mark the good beginning of the new year, and is popular in many parts of india and also a few countries but called in a different name. My bro-in-law was a mechanical engineer with a german based company and was a man with great sense of humour and takes good care of the most precious person in my life, there were times during my fights when I used to say things... Harsh things that would have ended most of the bro-sis relationship if it was someone else other then my sister, for me it was good that she was away from me and living with a person she loves and that person will take good care of her. As there was always a thought in me that if I ever became too rabid, If I become uncontrollable and cause nothing but pain to myself and those around me I could shoot myself down without causing harm to any more people and die with the satisfaction that the only person I care about in the world will live a happy life without me in it.

I reached my college and it was a usual day at work kind of day, the only difference was that I was chatting with amrita and bharat was looking at me in a weird way "what are you looking at??" I asked him in curiosity "bro I am sorry for what happened the other day" he said "you still think about that?? chillax bro." I said and resumed texting amrita "you texting amrita now right?? Dude there is something you need to know" before bharat could complete his sentence princi, ram and suresh sir barged into the library and shouted a few roll numbers including 122,123,134,197 and 223 which where the roll numbers of mine, Kiran, asif and bharat's. suresh looked at us with icy cold stares and shouted "if you don't get above 80% in the second preparatory then surely we will not give you the hall ticket" "you all come to the staff room we will make you understand in the only way you understand" princi said and escorted us to his chamber "oh..........fuck!" was all I could say before I got into the princi's chamber, but did manage to send amrita a text before leaving the library "dea my knuckles are gonna get broken...again so I won't be able to text you for now...... nothing unusual so don't worry and I will meet you in the library corridor in the lunch break..byee ;)"

INSIDE THE CHAMBER, as we waited outside our principle chamber and waiting for our turn to get canned, our princi and suresh sir had come out of the princi's chamber with four long wooden canes. It almost seemed like they enjoyed what they where about to do, suresh sir always had a ritualistic face when he held the two thick wooden cane in both his hands and escorted us to a place well secluded in the basement which is also used as a parking lot, or as we call it "the house of pain". I remember the first time when I was escorted there, it was during my first year in VCC. Because I was one of the many who couldn't get 85% in every subject that I had written and was considered fail. They used to take us as six or eight in a group, that is depending on the how much student 'failed' in their eyes. Inside, the 'house of pain' there will be about 10 lecturers, including the board members and some senior staff and they will be waiting to discipline us and make us get a very bright future. but all I ever got by their act was a really bright red mark on both my hands and knuckles.

"okay!! Roll numbers 122,123,134,197 and 223! You all come and stand here." the princi announced with his voice that trembled in his old age. There was no surprise in the way he arranged us. Me and most of my friends were together and that meant they were going to savour every moment they strike the long thick wooden cane on our body. "bro can I be honest with you all?? I am not even scared that we are going to get fucked up badly." bharat told all of us in a plain way, as if we were waiting to get some movie tickets in a long line. "I know dude!! First time is always scary and nervous. But we gain experience it won't be so tough" I said with a smirk on my face and we started walking to the basement. "you always think about sex or something?? I am a bit pissed off because even my own dad has not hit me bro!! and know these bastards are going to bang us badly!!!" asif said keeping his face down. His eyes had shrunk in and he had a pale face. "well bro!! porn is known to reduce stress and also it is believed to relive pain." I said and patted asif's shoulder. "So when Suresh hits you will you think of him as a hot chick. Dressed in black leather from neck to toe and imagine the wooden cane as a leather whip??" Bharat asked me and he had a faint smile on his face. "well suresh sir's wife is also a board member if she is there to beat the crap out of us then its fine." I said and all the guys in my group of six started laughing. "dude I think a dominatrix will at least spare her slave after some rounds!! But this bitch starts to break our bone after two or three rounds of profound torture." kiran commented and we burst out laughing. "oooh bro!! we are going to get fucked up today!! Like really bad aren't we??" asif asked me in a terrified tone. "what is this? the annual student torture ceremony??" I said with my mouth open. "fucking!! Helllll man!! There are like what twenty odd lecturers to punish us?" bharat managed to murmur. "it won't take me more than 15 minutes to burry those son's of bitches but I have to go through this just for a piece of paper." kiran told us, while princi allotted the lecturers accordingly to the number of students present there. "ooh fucking great. Asif! you and me are in great luck today man!! This is the maniac that is going to teach us discipline…our future is going to be really bright." I told him pointing at shekar, his eyes almost seemed to be filled with joy. we made our way to the secluded corner in the 'house of pain.'

"thiru and asif you both kneel down in the centre. Bharat and kiran over here and rest all just kneel down behind these two ghadha's" (donkey which is considered as a brainless animal)he said pointing towards me and asif. We had no other choice to keep our face down and fold our hands to our backs. "asif!! Bring your hands forward and tell all your subject marks one by one." shekar sir told him and stressed on the word one by one. "sir I got 89/100 in maths, 45/60 in physics,38/60 in chemistry and 32/60 in biology" asif told him and kept his face down. "hmmm 89/100 in math just pass. 45/60 in physics you shameless idiot how can you even tell your marks out loud?" shekar sir tells him and strikes the thick wooden cane on his knuckle. "sir what is this sir?? 45 /60 is more than enough. I have got 85 % in physics so why did you cane me?" asif asked him and made eye contact with him. "you dare back answer me??" shekar before completing his sentence slapped asif so hard that he almost fell on me, I was there on his right hand side. "what ever we are going to do now is for your benefit you won't understand it now and in the future you will." he told asif to go on and tell the rest of his marks. And as expected he found some or the other reason to strike him with his cane. "Bangalore boy!! Tell us your marks." Shekar sir ordered me and he himself brought my hands up in front of me. I always hated the nick name the lecturers had for me, even though I didn't think about it much it always reminded me that I was on stranger's land. "Sir Math 49/100, Physics 48/60, Chemistry 49/60, Biology 57/60" I said keeping my head down, I was prepared to get my knuckles broken. I thought I will get severely canned for just a subject and rest all will just pass away. "Lover boy here failed in Maths and Physics." he said and began to strike the wooden cane repeatedly on both my knuckles. I was shocked when he said the words 'lover boy' I didn't want anybody else to get hurt physically or mentally because of me, Just for the reason that they cared about me. It was that time when I realised it didn't matter how many marks we scored, rather didn't score. It meant that if we were escorted into the 'House of pain' nobody could save us from pain. "Sir I am sure that I passed in physics." I said and hoped that the canning would stop. After 15 canning or so he said "Specs thegi ley" (remove your glasses in kannada a language spoken in Karnataka.) After I did the same, I felt his hard right hand come flashing down on my left cheek. "Then what about Maths??" he said and started canning me on my back. All the while I was trying to control my emotions and tried not to look up into his eye's. "Why does that girl speak to you? That to she speaks to you!! A good for nothing waste of a human being." he said and waited for me to answer, the continuous canning had stopped. "Which girl sir??" I asked him with my shocked voice. "That girl to whom you were talking with that day in the corridor!! Don't pretend that you don't know. Already I heard some rumors about her, but after seeing her talk to you I am sure about it." he said and waited for me to answer him. "That's nothing sir. I just asked her for her physics record." I told him still keeping my head down. The tears that were struggling to come out of my eyes managed to release a few drops. "you just asked her for the record??shall I tell her name out loud?? Shall I tell it to Suresh sir? I thought you asked something else from her." he said with a cheap laugh along with his lab assistants. "That won't be needed sir. I just asked for her physics record." I said silently.

"You guy's should not get punished in such a closed place. You should be punished in the open in front of everyone so that other's see what happens if they don't follow our rules. Waran I am curious, if she watches you getting canned by me, what can she possibly do to stop me for hitting a useless idiot like you??" his cheap laugh grew louder. Even though I tried to control as much as I can, everyone could hear the vulgar way in which he asked me about her. That was the point I lost all my control, I knew I was going to get fucked up if I back answer him. But If I didn't do anything at that point of time, I would have never been able to look at amrita's face ever again. My breath became shorter and faster, maybe because I am asthmatic it usually happens to me when I face such emotions. "you are nobody to talk about her!!! You are nothing….." I said these words while tears where rolling down my eyes and I had a smirk on my face and I looked directly into his eyes. "you filthy form of life.. who do you even dare to do such stunts." shekar sir screamed at me, and caught my neck and applied pressure on it, maybe just for a few seconds. The next thing I know was that my face was on the ground and shekar sir was canning me repeatedly for I don't know how long. His lab rats made me to kneel down again and held my hands straight in front of me. Shekar sir would have enjoyed every moment of this as this time his strikes were not fast and repeated, it was slow and strong. During all this time, tears were rolling down my eyes but I never screamed. after sometime I didn't even feel the actual pain. I was imagining to be having the needle with me, and jabbing it onto his carotid artery. I wanted to see him bleed and choke him till the very moment, when his soul departs from his body. Even though all of it was just my imagination it gave me solace during my punishment. "hey! Leave him! If something happens to him, then it is a bad name to the school." My princi said and pushed shekar sir back. "you fools get out of here and try to pass in the pre board exams at least. Whatever we are doing here is for your own good" princi said looking at me. I was staring at the princi with my blood shot eye and my bleeding lips. Before I could say something, asif literally pulled me out of the basement. "nobody should know why that motherfucking shekar hit me so much, if they ask me the reason then needlessly amrita's life will become hell." I said washing away the blood with my hand kerchief. "just because of one girl you don't want to tell anybody about this??" bharat asked me curiously, and slipped a packet of cocaine out of his bag. he too got his fair share of beating. "not like that!! Even if I do tell my parents then they will come to fight with the management and then what happened with virat will happen to me. Then when the topic comes to why shekar hit me this badly, he will naturally tell them about amrita and all and needlessly her life will be more tough to live." I told him and went up to the library and took my place in one of the bench's in the corridor and kept my head on the desk and closed my eyes. I didn't want to speak to anyone, I just wanted to be left alone. "fuck...... my back and knuckles are fucking killing me. Thank god cocaine was created." I thought to myself, and snorted it in.

"Bharat is he in the library??" I could hear Amrita's voice asking for me and heard her footsteps getting close. I really didn't want to have a conversation with her, at that point of time. For all I knew, the only thing that existed between me and her was the 12th grade, high school love. That will be down the drain, as soon as high school gets over. "hi..... are you okay??" I started getting used to her care, which I sense most of the times when she speaks to me. "I am all cool. How was your day??" I asked her and try to keep a smile on my face. She was looking at me and didn't say a single word. "did you have your lunch??" she asked me after a long silence. "yup I just had.. what about you??" I replied her with a constant expression, that was stuck on my face. "get up now. We are going out." she told me and caught hold of my hand which I had placed underneath the desk. "aaah damnnnn.. okay sounds like a plan." I said and was about to get up, I really needed a break from the jail like environment. "what is all this? They hit you that bad uh?" she asked me and started to move her fingers over my knuckle. "it is just a token of love from princi. Need to apply some ice on it then it will be fine." I said and was looking around we any lecturer was heading our way. But no lecturer or peon or most of the students don't come anywhere near the top floor during the lunch hour. "let's go now.." she whispered in my ears and we headed down walking with our hands held. "hey bro?? coming to have your lunch or no?? and between amrita was looking for.." before he could complete his sentence he saw her with me and our hands were still held together. Bharat had a question mark on his face. Even though amrita tried to say a pleasant 'hi bharat' he didn't bother to even look at her face. "your friend has too much attitude. you know that right?" she asked me playfully. "not like that.. he doesn't get along with people in the beginning." we made our way to the parking lot. The same parking lot where I had spent the previous two hours of my day in a more than memorable manner. "hey amrita. We have a little bit of a problem. I don't have much fuel left. Can we take your ride instead??" I asked her a bit hesitantly. "that is not even a problem.. I will drive! hop on!" she said and moved to her moppet.

"so where do you want to go?? I am starving and we did to get back in an hour." "hmmmm there is a small hotel about ten minutes drive from here. We can get back on time." she said while slowly applying the torque on the accelerator. I was glad that she didn't say 'I don't know' like most girls I had been out with. "Tell me. What happened?? You look like hell." she said while caressing my knuckles. The whole journey from my school to the small fast food joint was quite, she did try to get me into a conversation. Maybe that was the coke, messing with my brains. But the more I heard her voice, the more I would see shekar sir in front of me and would visualize him talking crap about her. "what is this??" she almost screamed when she saw some dried blood on the corner of my lower lip. "its nothing! Just need to apply some ice and it will be fine." "no it is not fine!! That bastard hit you like an animal." she said and kept her thumb and index finger on my lower lip and started rubbing it. One positive attribute of this hotel was that it was of the olden day type, it had separate compartments to accommodate its guests and ensured their privacy. "it will be alright. Everything will, you are almost done here. Just a few days more." She said caressing my lips. "na not quite I don't see any possibility of things ending well for me." I was looking deep into her eyes when I was telling her how I felt. "it will be! I am sure it will be." she said and suddenly caught hold of my left shoulder and wrapped her hands around it, I could feel her warm cheeks on my shoulder. It felt warm, really warm. It felt although as if her cheeks were burning my shoulder. Suddenly I felt pain shooting up my shoulder, all though I wanted her hands wrapped around my shoulder. the pain was just too much to handle. She did sense my discomfort, she slowly rolled my half hand sleeves up, even I didn't notice that there were huge red cane marks and my parts of my shoulder were a little swollen. "ooh god!! You need to tell this to your parents.. you really need some medical help." Her voice was almost cracking and was staring at the 'mark of cane'. "naa chill I got it." I said and kept my forehead on hers. "answer this question honestly… are you taking some drugs??" she asked and took my hand in hers. "you are taking it right? You are high now! That's why you couldn't drive your bike. Well thiru, it is not that hard to figure it out. you love your bike more than yourself!!" she said and kept her soft lips were ever the marks were prominently visible. "let me feed you. Here open up 'aaaah" when she said 'aaaah' I could see that she opened her mouth as well and literally feed me a roti, which is a dish made of wheat. "now after school gets over.. you go to a doctor okay??" she said and rolled another piece of roti. "no ways I don't want this feeling to die. I want to feel the pain so that when I get him back, which I will. I can know the amount of pain he will go through!!" I said and swallowed another piece. "and how are you planning to do that??" she wrapped her hands over my shoulder. "well I am almost legally an adult but being a juvenile has its own perks in this country." I said and rolled a piece of roti and feed her. I could feel her soft lips brush against my fingers. "you might have done many horrible things in the past. But I know a bad guy when I see one. And you are not a bad guy at all." she said and eat another piece. "you really feel like that??" I asked her curiously. "every one has both good and bad within themselves. I am not sure how bad you are, but there is goodness in you." "every word you say to me. Everything you do for me is priceless!!" I said and placed my hands on her lips. "you are different than most people here. That's what I like about you. You always think different. But you said about that juvenile justice na? okay you won't be punished severely and even if you kill him you can come out of the correctional home within three years by many ways. but what about your life after that?? You won't get a seat in any reputed university, your family will think of you as a burden, people will speak shit about you. I have felt most of the things and trust me it hurts a lot" she said and placed her palm on my cheek. "look I don't care what would have happened to you in your past. But you mean everything to me now." I said and was looking dead straight into her eyes. "is it??" she said cheerfully and her lips widened and I was lost her hypnotic smile. "don't think that I am a control freak. But don't hangout with chiru much! He brings out the evil in you." she said with a huge smile on her face. "maybe if I stay in hubli long enough my name will turn into a name to be feared!!" I told her and caught hold of her hips from the side. "ooh yeah right!! Now lets go from here before we get too late." she said and got up. "how are you going to go home then??" she was a bit worried when she asked me about it. "bharat the savior will drop me home" I said and started walking towards her ride.

The rest of the day in school was pretty much normal, my gloomy mood had been long gone. Asif and bharat tried to make the day cheer full as much as they can. Kiran was just fucked up more than me. It so happened that the CEO suresh sir, princi and other board members hit the shit out of him and he got so pissed that he went away from school in the afternoon itself. Shekar sir even called me into the lab and said "whatever I did today was for your future only. Outside the classroom we all are like friends okay??" and presented a formal fake smile. "okay sir" I told him with an equally good fake smile. There was only one reason why he said those things to me, he had crossed the line when he was speaking about amrita and also crossed the teacher-student line when he practically hit the shit out of me. He was probably just scared of the consequences he must have to face If I had told the incident to my parents. But there was only one reason why I didn't say it to anyone. I wanted his blood on my hands, but thankfully for him my angel had brought me back before I stepped into hell. During my time in hubli, I did learn some things about the place and also learnt that there were few people there for me that would do anything I tell them to do and do it to anyone I tell them. One thing I gained from my days in the street apart from multiple fractures to various parts of my body was contacts. the type of contacts that were necessary for one to survive in hell. I am glad that I never crossed the line beyond a point. "hey bro!! were did you go with that....amrita man?? And why were you catching her hand?" bharat asked me in with a disgusted look.

"been to a small food joint! And why am I seeing so much disgust on your face?"

"she is like that man! I told you that day right?? She is not the good girl types!! she is a Area's slut!! And you fucker, I thought you didn't like her. I thought you liked her body!! Hell is wrong with you?"

"stop!!!! Don't ever say that. Yeah I just wanted to flirt with her, like most of the guys I wanted to date her. And have loads of fun with her! but now she is everything I got."

"fuck you bastard!! Then what about asif, me, Kiran and all of us man?? ek ladki aagayi tho ham sab gayab?! (you will forget all of us for some girl??)"

"you guys are the only reason why I could make it this far. but she, she gives the life to my life." I was beginning to loose my temper, I tried to end the conversation, because I knew that things were about to get out of hands.

"yeah 'life in my life' do you know how you sound?? Can you even hear yourself?? What did that whore do to you? She is a used maal (product) idiot!! Save the fucking speech alright??You don't even like second hand vehicles. Why are you behind her??"

"hey bharat!!! Enough man, you said enough….. go know!! And don't say things like that. She means a lot to him! Understand it." asif intervened and pushed us apart.

"yeah bhai!! More than us. He is behind that cheap slut. What did she show you?? Exposed her boobs to you, which many have groped!?? Or wait she removed everything just for 'you'?? noo!! Wait up I have a better idea. let me guess she let you fuck her?? Ooh I am sure she would have got fucked a hundred times by now at least."

"stopppp it!!! There are only a few living beings I can call as my friends! And you are one of them and trust me!! You………. Are……… fucking pushing it!!!" I said while pinning bharat to the wall and slamming my left fist inches away from his face.

"both of you shut up!! Go home and cool off!!! Bharat mad fuck!!! You need to undergo a professional course, that teaches you to speak to others properly!" asif said and pulled me back. Well I don't know if it was only with me, but if anything really bad happens to me. It occurs continuously and in series. "getting punished in the morning, badly bruised, fist which I thought was broken is broken now for sure and fighting with a best buddy!! Impressive it's a great day." I thought to myself.

Practical revisions

Our practical revisions started from the end of january, the winter in india was coming to an end. I don't know if it was because of the pressure but whenever I enter the street that leads to hell. I always felt extra heat and I would always break a sweat when I remove my helmet in the parking lot. Each and every friend of my were in different batches, I was in A-9. The fight between me and bharat got settled soon enough, asif played the judge and bharat kept telling me that he said what he said so that I won't get hurt further. It did a lot of explaining to him, and who else had a greater patience level then the monk asif. My first practical revision was for physics, luckily isha was in the same batch as I was. and that was a relief to me and I was glad to see her. I was a little late that day so I was forced to share a table with two other guys who basically performed every experiment and I didn't quite get a proper chance to revise the experiments. my two hours of practical revision went away very quick and I did not do anything much the whole day.

"hi isha!!its quite awesome that you are in the same batch as mine.. because even during our board practical we will be in the same batch" there was a huge grin on my face. "yeah!! Nice to see you to!!how was your revision? and did you get your records corrected??" she asked me with a pleasant smile. "well actually my phy, chem. and bio records are yet to get corrected" I told her with a mischievous smile. "why????? Get it corrected fast or you will be in trouble." She said a bit concerned, she always had a dead zombie face whenever she was angry, sad and concerned. "I know that. Let this hall ticket probs get cleared..i'll get it corrected within tomorrow.." I tried to make it sound as politely as I could. "so not going home??" "no yar. I will sit in the library and read here itself." she said looking at nagraj, our tall dark and lean librarian with a temper. "with that nagu staring at you and the princi observing your every moves!! I feel like I am in a reality show when I am in that place." I told her pointing towards the sliding glass door which is the grand entrance to the solitary confinement. "seriously!! Enjoy it bye!!" I taunted her. "bye!!" she said and waved at me. I was rushing down the fleet of stairs when I saw my angel coming up the stairs. "hiiii.. have a great day and enjoy your chem revision" I told her and continued to walk down the fleet of stairs. "hey wait!! Why in such a hurry??" she asked me surprised. "I've to give something to a friend and he is waiting for me now.." I told her with my never ending smile on my face. I have no idea why though, it just appears on my face whenever I look at her. "fine.. will see you later" she said and started walking up the fleet of stairs, I was completely lost in the way her hips moved from side to side as she walked up. "do text me when your practical get over" I said her, still lost at her hip movements. she noticed it, she turned her head back and smiled at me.

I managed to go to bharat's house within minutes. And horned, 3-4 times standing in front of his house. "wait up dude I am coming" he screamed from inside his house. "don't come out and all!!! I am coming in." I shouted and parked my ride outside his house. "the merchandise is waiting and is brand new come fast." he said as I was removing my shoes and socks in one go and barged into his house. "here 8GB memory card.. Give your latest collection right now!!" I said flashing a small memory card to his face. "I didn't even speak properly to amrita man..load the card with hotties." I said and turned on his laptop. "you are the only guy to rush from school to my house and covered two kilometers in less than 5 mins, and in the process didn't even speak properly to the girl you kissed a few days back." bharat said with his eye brows raised. "do not look so surprised fucker. Last month we used 5 GB of your internet to watch brandi love and lisa ann hits!! And not to mention doctor adventures." I said and plugged in the hardware. "good old times…even if I don't become an engineer.. I will try to become a cameraman for brazzers." bharat told me with a wicked grin and opened his secrete folders. nobody can get their hands on those files except bharat himself. "you are an addict and so am I…so which one do you want? Blonde, ebony or latina??" he said while he was searching for his new collections. "latina chicks are hot and get me those indian MMS clips as well, the one with good clarity." I said and picked my choice of videos. "MMS yup! Always fun to watch. natural stuff no acting." bharat said and loaded the memory card. After a while of chatting I was going to take leave from his place and was hoping to get my records corrected. "cheers all the best for your practical revision." I said and raced away to my house.

"bro from tomorrow we won't have any practical revision. And we have to write the re-exam tomorrow itself it seems."

asif was screaming from the other end of the phone. "what the fuck bro?? we just wrote it like a week ago!! Damn bro the cane marks are still fresh on my back and again we have to write it??how are they expecting us to pass if they tell us all of a sudden??" I was pissed at the entire world. "when I asked suresh sir the same thing. he told me not to write the board exams and to directly write the supplementary exams in june." asif said and was still screaming on the other end. "this is just so damn unfair!!" I said and hung up. After 10 mins or so I got another call from bharat about the same matter. He was upset anyone could make it out by his voice. the re–exam was sailed through with a lot of hard work and making sure we don't get caught copying. After the re-exams in math and physics, we were relaxed and were expecting study holidays for a month or so because we got to know that our practical were postponed. but instead our school cancelled everyone's practical revision classes and informed us about the commencement of the second pre boards which started in a week's time. "I am really beginning to doubt if they want us to write the board exams or want us to quite" asif said with his sad gloomy face. we felt like our balls were kicked with a brand new F50I studs.

2nd preparatory boards

"dude there is no hope for CET(common entrance test) man" bharat told our gang of four, who were seated in the four corner of the wooden table with a glass cover on top of it. "bro correct me if I am wrong, but aren't we sitting in the library past four months because our school management thinks that we will fail in our boards" I taunted bharat, whenever we used to land in a tough situation. It was always fun to taunt bharat, because compared to all of us. he was the one to get banged most number of times. "forget CET and all..... but our college should give us sometime to study right???" asif said while removing his cool leather jacket. "I think there is some scam going on here. every student should write the second pre board or only the students dying, sorry I mean studying in the library?" D.K asked me with a sarcastic smile. "arrey bhai (hey brother) each and every student should write it" I told him with surity. "guys I don't want to be de-meaning but, I think I am going to fail in the pre boards this time also" bharat told us and kept his typical bharat special worried look on his face. "you will never know how good a girl is unless you...." Asif didn't complete his sentence. "leave it man. looking at your face itself I know what you will do with a particular girl" D.K interrupted him. "I meant you can never know how good a girl is unless you talk to her...so you will never hit a hat-trick unless you try to shoot." asif told bharat with a determined face. Nobody said I single word after that. Because most of the people in the library were in the same condition that I was in, no matter what I tried or what I do everything led me to failure. After a point of time when one is deprived of success worth the effort they put in. they begin to question themselves if they are good enough or are they a complete waste of a human life. We were all dead serious about the up coming days, as one thing was clarify we screwed up in any test by any margin. then its good bye hall ticket, which meant that two years in hell was rat shit.

Our first exam was chemistry and as usual it went well. The next exam was physics, we had a gap of two days to study for it. But thing was we didn't know what the hell should we study from, because while most of the schools bring up questions from the state government prescribed books. Our school like many other private schools, who are solely behind fame and money never even bothered to teach us anything from the textbook. There is no wonder why students from less privileged background, studying in a government school top the board exams majority of the times. It is not only because they don't have a smart phone or not because they don't have a facebook account. for many parents in india take pride in telling others, that their kids are studying in a top private school in the city. Some pay a fortune as donations to enroll their kids to these hell holes. And slowly the harassment in such places goes unheard off. It is natural for every parent in the world to think of their 17 year old teen as a mischievous brat. But after a period of time, majority of the parents around the world make sure whether some thing wrong is happening in their life. But that is never the case in india, here we are said to follow a traditional culture and the teenagers and young adults who are broad minded towards any situation, are often treated as aliens by our elders. Here even a final cry for help by a young adult is seen as a tantrum. In schools like mine, they needlessly focus on the refrence book. "if we study the theory perfectly and practice the derivation, then we can score well bro" I was pacifying D.K who was sobbing on the other end of the line, mostly he was drunk as well. "bro! again I am going to fail, my parents will again kill me by their words. You know I work for a gangster on part time basis right?? I am thinking of going along with them bhai." he said sobbing for most of the sentence and laughing when he said the last few words. "don't ever say that!!! You are better than those scumbags." I told him slowly, the last few words he said, brought up some bad memories from the past. "Is that how you go to sleep every night?? Telling yourself you are better than those people." he was laughing uncontrollably "you are the worst form of life to walk the face of the earth. arrey bhai you are way worse than those people but you have some misplaced sense of self righteousness. when your life turns into hell, when you are not permitted to write the BOARD EXAMS, the same motherfucking exam that changed my life to hell. Then you burn them down with your anger. You beat them up till you are satisfied, and when you do. then come and join us, we will make sure that you walk away untouched." He said still sobbing in some point of the sentence and laughing during the rest of it. "what ever bro.. you are completely drunk. Don't worry man!! Asif and bharat managed to talk to naidu sir and they got some question banks from which the question will come." I told him with my trembling voice. "and I don't lie myself to sleep.. I take a shot of pink vodka every night." I said and hung up.

"man how did you manage to get your hands on this?? And what is this??" I asked bharat and flashed a whole bunch of white and black printed sheets on his face. "naidu sir resides near to asif's house. And these are delhi CBSE board model question papers." Bharat said with disappointment. "how can we possibly pass this one?? We are from karnataka state board!!there is absolutely no way that we can get through it" I told bharat nervously. "well I am sure we are in some game, where we can never walk out of this hell" bharat said looking pale. "what will be the benefit of the college if we don't pass uuh??" I wanted to make him believe that we still had a chance, I was sure that we were done. But as asif always tells 'you can not score a hat-trick if you hesitate to shoot'. "bro D.K wants to meet up" bharat said and walked towards my bike. "that bro is mad. Lets get him a copy of this shit as well" I said and kick started my beauty. "already done. Lets go to KMC ground" he said and hoped on my ride.

"slow down bro!!!!!!!! how the fuck does amrita sit behind you man??" he was screaming near my ear over the thick plastic of helmet. "it is 6.30 in the morning and not a living soul is on the road.. did you really expect me to not drive the way I am driving now??" I said and started tilting my bike from side to side. After a while D.K arrived with his 25 year old 'CD 100' I loved the way he maintained it, I always love the vintage bikes. "I am sorry about the other day man! I was not in control of myself" D.K said and lighted his cigar. "no problem brother!!!!! Here just read this. It is quite easy, you can pass easily, by pass I mean 'VNC' level of pass. "really sorry man and thanks." D.K said and started to go through the paper which had a few solutions on them as well. "dude if anybody gets to know all the answers then let me know." D.K told bharat, and let out a huge puff of smoke. "I am feeling really bad man. Is there anything I can do to make it up to you??" D.K asked me with a guilty look on his face and sucked in another puff. "it is really no problem. but because you insist we can race against each other." I told him with a smile on my face. "what really?? I am totally broke man." he said and emptied his pockets. "you can personally tune my bike. Slow down the throttle a little, and do it absolutely free of cost." I told him and waited for his reply. "you do know why we call him DK right?? He is the best" bharat told me with amusement. "precisely the reason why I want it." I said calmly. and for D.K it was a welcoming challenge "don't think that I will go easy on you." he said and lighted another cigar.

Back home, I tried to understand the bunch of paper in front of me. But what I could do wasn't enough. it was around 11.30 am when I called bharat and explained him about the situation I was in. after a while of laughing, the kind of laughter we get when we know that our friend is also going to get screwed big time along with you. He replied that he was also in a similar one. And he couldn't understand most of the paper. We were not in the situation because we were brainless idiots, it was because of a simple reason that the syllabus thought in karnataka state board was no much for the syllabus thought in CBSE board. "what the fuck can a state board guy do, when he is given a fucking CBSE paper to prepare for that to in less than a day??" I told him and before I could vent out some more steam. "bro lets go to the edge of the city. And you kill me dude, I will be very happy if you do that" bharat said annoyed. "if I kill you then who will kill me you fucker?? Try to study how much ever you can" I said and hung up. I got another call as soon as I hung up. "hey man.. did you manage to figure the paper out???" I asked DK. "fuck that bro. I got so pissed after looking at it. does our school want us to quit!! Do they want us to say words like 'sir I can't study for the boards in such a short time, I will write the re exam in july'?? DK asked me and anyone within a six mile radius could hear him. "chill bro.. where are you now??" "I am simply roaming the city in my car." he replied plainly. "is it a race or joy ride??" "no not a race just driving casually." he said and could hear some car's horn and a whistle sound mostly by the traffic cops. "okay bye bro!! and whatever you do don't be absent for the exam, just write it for formality at least" I told him and tried to sound convincing. "I will see that" was his immediate reply.

Practical Exams

After yet another disappointing finish to my preparation. I flunked in math and physics, thank goodness the practical started after two days of our incredible performances. I was in the morning batch along with isha, my first practical exam was physics and I was nervous. but I already knew what to expect as bharat had his physics practical a day before me. I cleared all my doubts with him and called him in the middle of the night to clear some points about the experiments and practiced them till late night. I was high on confidence and I didn't have time to revise just one of the twelve experiments.

I reached my school and hurried up the fleet of stairs to the top floor of the building. I saw virat and chiru, were just chilling out. while others were just doing the nerdy stuff of revising their manuals. Around 7.45 am suraj and shiva sir came out of the lab to give us a vote of confidence. It was around 8.00 am when we all saw our 6.2"ft tall giant external, who had seen me chatting with isha. And he had a look which said 'hey kiddo you are going to be my bitch for the next two hours'. Shiva sir was my internal in charge and he made us to stand in a line and pick our chits at random on which the name of the experiment to be performed were written. I still do believe that satan himself was watching over me and to my luck I had got the experiment 'refractive index of concave lens'. The same experiment that I was not perfect with. "sir can I take another chit??" I asked shiva sir quietly. "no you can't but we will take care of you don't worry, and pretend that you are doing something" he told me slowly and rushed me to go near my allotted place. As I walked towards my allotted table, I had a sick feeling in my gut. "not like the first year practical please!" I thought to myself and started my experiment with the standard procedures and with every round of inspection by the external examiner, I pretended that I was doing something. I got all the help from shiva sir and I managed to complete the rest of the experiments. It was around 9.45 when a few other externals had come for inspection. "sir! Did you have your breakfast?? Lets go have it now" shiva sir asked them politely and led them out. I submitted my paper along the experimental results. And suraj sir didn't bother to ask me any viva questions "hey look go out now!! And if someone ask's you just say that you answered all your viva questions" he said and rushed me out. Maybe bharat was right. Even though we spent four months in the library we got really close with the lab technicians. My chemistry practical was good enough. Day's passed when I had to face my enemy shekar sir and my biology practical was next. Even to get my biology record corrected was a huge war of words. But I had to stand and take everything he threw at me. And finally he took my register number, batch name and date of my practical and told me to get lost, almost as if playing a mind game with me and to make me think that he was planning something big for me. The very reason of which I had to prepare myself for a hard touchdown. I met nashi and took the question paper from him, it's a good thing that it's the same set of questions for every batch. And I also had a run through the procedures and also cleared a few doubts. "relax dude!! Don't be so tensed. You look like you are going to have a stroke" he said with his classic smirk on his face. "I am not tensed man. just preparing for the worst possible situation before hand" I replied him, and was going through the set of questions. "isn't that called being paranoid??" he taunted me and was texting someone. "well you got a point there. But that motherfucker is going to target me. you know that right?" I told him and was going through the procedures in the manuals. I left his house around 6.00 in the evening and went over to my place and managed to by heart each and every experiment I had. after my experience in physics, I was determined to leave no stone un turned.

It was late evening when I had discovered that my slid was broken, rather had a slash in the top left corner, my initial gut was that it's fine its not a big problem, but somewhere behind my head I always had a thought about it. I then called up nashi to borrow his dissection box, and by borrowing I mean taking it and never returning it back. "hey fucker!! You were in my place sometime ago. you could have taken it that time itself right?? I am out now, will call you after I reach home and do not panick!!!" the last sentence he told me was loud and clear.. I did keep my cool for about 15 mins but then I called up praveen, a nerdy guy that was near my house and a one of the few people that I could call as a friend. "bro. is your bio practical over?? Can I borrow your dissection box??" I asked him and tried to sound as polite as I could. "yes dude..do you want it??" he asked me with a geeky voice. "yes bro.. I'll be there in front of your house in

10 minutes or so" I told him and grabbed my bike keys and rushed down towards my bike. "drive slow" my mom said with that typical motherly care. "come out bro I am outside" I texted him and was waiting outside his house, I never had a habit of going over and ringing the bell and greeting an unknown stranger who may open the door. "fuuck you idiot!! You should stop doing that." praveen told me with his not so geeky voice, I was standing in a dark corner near his house and when he walked past me. I silently keep my bike keys behind his neck. "you are standing here like some fucking moron who is on the street to mug some people." he said and recovered his breath. "awww did I scare the scientist??" I mocked him and collected his dissection box for good. And also cross checked the entire procedure with him. Maybe I was paranoid? Even I didn't know that I had such a side in me. "thiru I am free now. Come home man" nashi said over the phone. "free now?? What the fuck were you doing man?? Makin out with that mysterious person you text??". "you want your precious slide or no man??" he mocked me, or so he thought. "I got the entire set from praveen man" I replied him with a swag. "after you done with the practical. Google the word P-R-A-N-O-I-D" he said and was laughing simultaneously. "I'd rather google for naughty America". "fuck off you porn addict. And good luck dude. and also don't mind what shriek sheky tells you. For two hours he owns you and after that time period you can do anything you want to him." "okay bro thanks will keep that in mind!!good night man." I told him and was about to hang up. "you are not going to sleep but yeah G N" he told me and hung up, nashi always uses the short form of

such words. I just revised one last time before a heard some soothing songs of the eagles, linkin park and dosed off.

And finally the moment I was preparing myself for had arrived. I left my house extra early at exactly at 7.30 am, I could feel my hand getting numb. I never knew whether it was the nervousness or my over speeding in the streets during the winter of january. the cold winds were hitting my face so harshly that it reminded me the canning from shekar sir, it was the only time in my life when I put down my gyser and covered my face completely. I parked my bike right next to where isha had parked her moppet. And rushed up to the third floor from the basement, while I crossed the house of pain. One thing struck my mind, if he throws everything he had on me and if I was still standing, he would be weaponless in front of me. I don't know how I got the surge of positivity, maybe it was my paranoid preparation or maybe it was the text from amrita I got in the morning. "may I come in sir??" I asked a tall and lean figure across the room. "get in" a feminine voice replied from behind the stocks of closets, it was mumtaz man, a really sweet teacher, she let asif copy some answers after he got his corrected paper and made sure that he passes. well asif always has a guardian angel over his head. Then I finally saw the devil. Shekar sir, he was dressed in his usual attire. He was wearing his typical brown shirt and karkhi pants. He was looking at me as though he ws awaiting me. I was irritated by his cold icy stares and I kept telling myself "two hours!! Just two hours or less just take the pain and once you get out of the room he is your bitch". my practical exam went really good with some help from mumtaz mam and also my paranoid practice paid off.. I wasn't sure about one answer and as I was in clear view of the external examiner, who was also asif's distant relation. I had no choice to ask shekar sir. :pentacular aestivation" he told me the answer silently and went away. I was star bound, is that one text from amrita that powerful and meaningful? the rest of the experiment was all good and time had come for every 12th graders nightmare, it was time for the viva question asked by the external examiner. I saw the way isha was getting screwed by the external examiner and again recollected amrita's text, I had no clue why I had read that text so many times. it was just of two sentences. "one last step and I don't have come inside that filled room ever again" I thought to myself and it was my turn to answer the viva question. "good day mam." I told her with a pleasant smile. "yeah good day sit down." she replied adjusting the thick pair of glasses that she wore. since I was the only guy in my batch, she didn't ask me any difficult questions and just told me to explain my experiment to her orally. I did answer all her questions related to the experiment and got up from the steel chair in front of the external examiner. "I basically did everything in this experiment to him mam, and look at his handwriting!! he has to work really hard." he said and picked up the paper which was near the external. "mam he wasn't even near me, I was directly in front of you during the whole experiment. he has some personal grudge against me mam." I said and extended my hand, asking him for my paper and didn't make any eye contact with him. After examining the paper again he handed it over to the external while I still had my hand stretched out near him. Mumtaz mam, signaled me to go out and so I followed, I didn't even take my corrected record back, I left it there in the same formaline stench filled room. Maybe he Is still having it now, and using it as a bad example in front of my juniors. on the way down I caught up with isha who seemed a bit upset. "did the mean examiner upset the lil baby??" I asked her and nudged her shoulders. "shut up yr!! I am in tension" she said while walking down the fleet of stairs that led us to the parking lot. "don't worry .." I said and walked to my bike. Her moppet was just beside mine. "hey thiru stop that!!!!!" isha commanded me in fear, I was doing a standing burnout and made sure that the sweet sound between rubber to bitumen spread across the level of floors. "amrita hates it when you do such things." she said with a slight smile on her face. "there is no major risk in doing this at all." I said and increased the torque on my accelerator. "you have no idea how afraid she gets when she see's you doing such crazy stuff." she said looking down at the burning tyres. "yeah?? Tell me about it" I said and stopped my stunt. And isha started her moppet. "no! really tell me about it."

All roads lead to this

All roads did not lead to the much needed study holidays. We were just a month away, from our board exams. It rather lead us to a very narrow and dangerous path. Suresh sir and princi called us to assemble on feb 10th in hall number 4. And then they instructed our routine for the next 'few days', we had attend important classes for math and physics and then we will be writing a test on it the very same day. It was just a course of six days. Three days for Physics and three days for Math and we had to perform really well to earn our hall ticket. Our simple six day crash course lasted till march 4th. Only two students who I was shocked to see in the slow learner class had managed to earn the hall ticket, and also a week's time to prepare for the board exams. There were around sixteen people who didn't get the hall ticket, which is illegal for the school to with held the hall ticket without any valid reasons. I, Asif, Bharat and DK were the one of the many who were not given their soul right. On 5th of march we all were informed to assemble in the princi's chamber. we were waiting out in front of the office. "Don't be so tensed also man. chill you did well, we did some incredible team work. So if I get the hall ticket so will you." Asif assured me and our school receptionist had called us one by one with a mark sheet in her hand. "see bro I got it man. And will you." Asif said showing his white paper with a blue ink print on it.

"My roll number was highlighted and she told me to meet the princi now. "No way!! I have got good marks in both the subject you people tell I am weak at. Get me the hall ticket now." I almost threatened her, I had a huge fight with my parents and sis the previous night for the same reason. "You have to meet the principal I can't give you the hall ticket, its with Suresh sir." The old lady with tobacco stained teeth told me uneasily. "Then what the hell is that?" I said pointing at my hall ticket which she held in her hand. "I am sorry but you have to meet sir." she said calling the next roll number. "Sure I will" I grunted back at her. Next it was Bharat's turn, when he found out that his roll number was not highlighted he was on cloud 9 to the hard ground below. Me and bharat were being lead to the princi's room by our royal escort, the CEO himself.

My left hand was shaking continuously and it was not from fear, It was because of anger. "dude I need it… please get me a packet, dude give it." I was pleading him for a pack of cocaine. Bharat clearly refused to give it to me. "I am just 17 years old, I am a juvenile. I can kill these two bastards with my bare hand. I can stick my pen so deep into his eye socket, and savour the his screams when the pen enters his brain." I said bharat in whispers and waited for princi to come in along with suresh sir. "thiru?? Your eyes are getting squint man." Bharat said in his trembling voice. "see bharat!! you didn't even pass once also in math. It is better if you write your exam in june." suresh sir said looking seriously quite. "thiru, its better if you do the same." "no sir!! I showed you my improvements I worked for this, without doing or caring about anything I worked for this!" I argued. "yes I know, but I think you want to do medicine no? you have the potential its better if you write in june. start attending 2nd PUC classes from 13th, I will tell all the teachers to give you personal attention to both of you." CEO said this was the first time, I saw a smile on his sadistic face. "okay!!!!" bharat screamed at them and walked out of the room crying. "no sir. I worked for it, I showed you the results I need this." I argued, I think the word beg will be more appropriate. "write in june if you want or don't write it at all. but you are finished! you can leave now." princi said with a sadistic grin over his toothless face. I almost felt that he enjoyed doing it to me. I barged out of the room and explained the entire situation and screamed over the phone. "thankss!!! thanks alooooooooooot. I can never have my life back!! How can you expect me to face other people back home again??" and tears running down from the corner of my right eye. call uncle and tell him to force my school to give the fucking hall ticket now" I screamed back at her. "no don't want that. I'll tell dad to handle it. you concentrate on your boards, we will make sure you accept it" she told me calmly. "what exams??? It's the end!! your father can't do anything about it... As princi said I am finished" I said and switched off my phone. "HEY you!! come inside the prinicpals room." suresh sir said and took me in. for a second, I thought that they will drop the act, and hand over the fucking piece of paper. "look thiru. you have got good marks in your practical. I can make you get out of out in these." princi sir said with a charming smile. "I am listening." I said indifferently. "we will call your dad in the afternoon and you have to come. In front of him just say that you can't study for the board exams in such short period of time. And we will help him understand your

potential, we will provide special coaching to you for free."
princi said keeping his hands on my shoulder. My mind was
fixed on a text I received from amrita sometime ago, it read
'two things can never be long hidden for you, your passion
to achieve things you want and to achieve the things you
had the passion for.'" is it what the text mean?? It means bull
crap! What the hell am I even worth? It ends here." I thought
to myself. "when I go home now, I will scream at my mom
and when dad returns home I will confront him and over
power him, like yesterday's night. After some days my sister
will stop picking my calls. My mom will regret giving birth
to me and my powerful and influential dad will be in utter
disgrace to have such a son like me." random thoughts were
flooding my mind usually the people who are suicidal, are
weak and don't care about there family. but if I am alive.
Things will be fine for a week maybe, but what about the
week after that? Slowly I will be blamed for not coping up
with the pressure, soon I will just be a liability to everyone
that cares about me... that used to care about me." It was
that moment, that I decided to end every pain and suffering
I had. How much ever I tried and how much ever I got hit
and tormented was going for a waste. that fact killed me
from within. "my dad will surely meet you." I said and
withdrew myself from his grip and walked out of the door.
"hey!! Sir is calling you" a peon held my hand and stopped
me from going out. "kai theeeeeeegi ley (get you hands off
me)" I said and didn't look back, I am not even sure if It was
the peon that caught my hand.

I rushed down towards the staircase, that led me to the
parking lot. "thiru!!! Wait!! can't you hear me??" a feminine

voice screamed at me and forcibly held my hand. I did not say anything or look back, rather I took my hand back by force. Every moment of life which I had in the sunshine was flashing in front of me. I was in that point of life, when I wanted to close my eyes and didn't want to wake up at all. I preferred to stare at the never ending darkness, then the harsh truth behind it. "look at me thiru." the same feminine voice that seemed too familiar repeated again and caught my hand with force. "what the fuck do you want??" I said and withdrew my hand back and I looked at her soft hands, that was still trying to hold me. It was amrita, one good thing about the library was that even in its sick environment, it attracted her to study in it. "what happened??............ Let's go from here!!" she said and held my shivering left hand. "let me take my bike!! I have to go some where now. it is place that I was waiting for a long time to be in." I said and started walking again. "no lets have a walk. Don't you want to walk with me??" she said with a care that has no words to describe. "I do! I wish I could do.......... But I really got to go. I need something." I whispered into her ears and started walking away from her. It was the worst ever feeling in my life, here my best but the least possible future wanted to go on a walk with me. While I was walking to my destined future. But she didn't let me go, she started to scream at me and did a lot of things which attracted the attention of many. She forced me out of the parking lot, the only reason why I agreed to walk away from the prison was so that the situation goes away unreported to others. We were holding hands the whole time, that was such a high school thing to do so. "now say slowly!! What happened" she asked with a caring smile. I told her everything that had happened in the past two hours and the fight I had last night. "don't worry our school is doing a major scam. You don't break okay??" she said and was still holding my hand. "no!!! I am done!! I am finished I want to dieeeeee!!!!!!!!!!!! I need it…. I need some coke, please call bharat tell him I need some cocaine. Call him please I will die without it, I want to dieeeeee" I said like a mad man and pushed her hand away. "thiru you are better than that! You don't need it…. You are not thinking straight what about your family??" she asked me calmly. "what fucking family??? It is because of them I am here in the first place!! They didn't understand that I was getting tortured here every………dayyyyy. For them my final cry for help was a tantruuuuum" I said and was extending the second last letter of every word I said. "that is not what they meant…they have a dream for you…and your eyes what is wrong with them??" she said and try to come near me. my right eye was full of tears and I pushed her away again, this time I pushed her chest away. "fuck the word family!! When I am dead they will cry for five days that's it, sooner or later they will move one with their lives. Maximum a photo of me with a garland will be hung in some corner of my house and when they miss me they will cry but eventually they will forget me. my sis might miss me more at times, she might even think it was her fault that I died, but even she will eventually try to forget that I was ever in her life. Maybe, its better if I die, I only cause pain to the people I love." I said and began to move my head from side to side. "hey thiru your eyes…your eyessss" she had a worried look on her face and was looking straight into my eyes. "well its better if …." "your eyes are getting squint." she said and the next thing I felt was her hard right hand slapping me repeatedly, the slap was so powerful that my spectacles went flying away from my face. "nooot true noot true at all!!!! Don't even think about such things. I have been where you are!! I have felt what you have felt to end your own life. It is never the way!!! You say nobody cares for you?? Just switch on your phone and see how many missed calls you would have got from the people that care. this who you are now?? an animal that is too hurt and wants to kill itself? You think I don't care about you? Then you are very wrong and you haven't been so wrong in your entire life, that has so much potential. Face the truth! I care about you! And yet you pushed me away, like I am some worthless piece of paper? All that because you want to die?............ look at yourself now! You are a worthless drug addict, too afraid to bare the pain??" she was catching both my wrists hard, just so that my hands will stop shaking. "yesss!!!! I am nothing more then a drug addict!! See you mean the world to me here! And yet I pushed you away....like a piece of paper, you say that I am too afraid ... no I am not, this is what that is left of me. You said it yourself I have become an animal, that is too hurt. My life is over! I can except that. Everything ends in life, and this is the only way the sorrow of my life ends. Please let me get the one thing I want the most............." I could not dare to look at her eyes, I was sobbing my sorrows away. "and please can you do me a favor??? Just tell bharat to tell my sis that it is not her fault and that I want her to live a really happy life ok? She has suffered a lot, just because she is my sis. And to tell my parents that........... tell them that I am sorry for everything and….. uuuh and……..screw it! goodbye amrita!" I said and freed myself off her. I wanted to take my own ride for a final masquerade. I wanted to feel the fresh breeze of air hit my face, I wanted to remove my helmet and hit the top gear. Then I would free my hands of the handle bar and raise above to brace my final impact, mostly with an oncoming speeding truck. It was not the easiest way to go. But that was the only way I thought of.

I never meant to say those things to her, I didn't want her to feel that I was a weirdo in the last conversation of my life. But I really wanted to say it to someone, by luck she was the one. I looked at her tear filled eyes for the last time and turned my back. "maybe if I spied at her one last time, I could have seen those eyes that smile for her. I did want to hear my mom's always caring voice, she used to panic if I turned up home late. I wanted to hear my sister's voice again, I knew that she will never forgive me for what I was about to do. It felt weird that I even wanted to hear my dad's voice, my dad even though he always had that strict, over protective look. I knew that he was soft and caring as any other dad. Every step I took, I could remember the happiest moments of my life with my family. The small fights with my sis to decide which TV show we should watch, I was the one that used to win. I could remember the nights when I was in seventh grade and used to get unexpected asthma attacks, and my dad would rush me to a near by hospital. I didn't want to die, I wanted to live happily. Which I never could, I entered the street to hell. I wanted to look back at amrita again, hug her tight and tell that I love her. I wanted to tell her how much solace I had been in, when I was with her. I just wanted to die, not because I was to afraid to face the reality, it was because I wouldn't live in the reality and harm everyone that cared about me. It is not at all the right thing to do…. I don't have a choice" I was sinking in my own thoughts. And turned on my phone, I wasn't sure what I should speak to my family. I was sinking in my own thoughts. "wait you bastard!!! look at me now!!" amrita caught my collar and pulled me back, she was breathing heavy and there was sweat on her forehead. "you want to die? Because you say that you are not worth living your life, that you can't take six more months of torture? You fucking think your life is tough?? then come to terms with the actual reality. Everyone's life is broken in one way or the other. For me….. for me…… People think I am a slut here!!! People treat me as a slut!! And this started to happen so rapidly that I would feel myself sinking in. I was a kid back then, I was in love with the whole ideology of being in love. I got used and used so much that there is no going back for me." she told me with some tears rolling down her cheeks. I didn't have any courage to look at her. I wiped the dirt of my glasses. I had got 7 missed calls from my sis and three texts from her. And four missed calls from asif and bharat each. I tried to look at her and was ashamed to make an eye contact. "you think your life is too tough to live and that you die everyday?? Then wake up! You are not the only one with a tough life!!! The guy who I was in love with for the first time in my life, I placed all my trust in him. I believed that he was my prince. I was in a dreamland with him. I would believe everything he said, every time he said that he will never leave me, I felt like I was the most important thing in his life and that made me feel special. But do you know what did he do to me?? he cheated me, made me sleep with him. I hate drugs…. It is just so easily available to everyone, He added some drug in my drink and filmed me on his bed. he even started spreading the video when I refused to sleep with him again, he forced himself with his friends on me. I had to catch his legs and beg him! Even though I felt like killing him……….. I had to beg that pig so much that he deleted the video along with the replica's. but still people get to know things. And they didn't make my life any easy to live. You may ask how am I still alive and face our society?? am I a slu….??" before she could say any other word I placed my thumb on her lips. "ssssh!! stop please stop.. don't get hurt again!! Because of me." I said and caressed her lips with my thumb. "forget about mine. this is not the way I wanted to tell you about it." she said and wiped away her tears. "you never had to.." I had got a call from my dad, I was hesitating to pick it up. "just pick up!!!" she said and tapped on the receive button, I didn't have an android phone. "uuuuh thiru?! …… Don't worry. I made some arrangements and your school has agreed to give you your hall ticket, I just have to meet them in the noon." my dad said with his rough typical manly Indian voice. "see when your dad has so much influence why don't you just use it??" amrita said wiping away her tears. "this was the third time I spoke to my dad in two years!" I told her with a faint smile on my face. "so still want to die you idiot??again as I said many times don't think that you're the only one with a tough life. And running away from your life is never an answer. I hope you understand that now….." she said still catching my hands, the shivering had stopped reasonably. "thanks for everything I am sorry." "all cool now?? I can go back and study??" she came near me and hugged me tight. "the slaps were hard……. Really hard but necessary!!! And really sorry for the way I treated you." I said, I had never felt such a guilt in my whole life.

Even though my outburst episodes were quite common for my family, I didn't loose mind to such an extant. Amrita was not even my family, she tried to control me, when even my own mom would have been scared to come near me. "just be cool. you will get through.. remember the text I sent you??" she asked playing with my hairs. "I am really sorry!! It will never happen again." I said and kissed the side of her cheek. this was the first time I was appreciating the location of my school, once anyone crosses the street that lead us to hell. it was just unoccupied acres of land that surrounded it.

"it is weird you know…"

"what's weird??a guy crying in front of a girl??" she tells as a slight smile appeared on her lips. "and stop doing that stupid drugs will you?? It changed you for what you are."

"no.. well yeah!! It is hard.. but that's not it….. it's weird that I always think about this day…….. I have imagined this day a million times in my head, on what I'll say and what I'll do when every step I take leads to a failure. and every single time I think about this day, I try to erase the worse possibility and fill it with something better….but now when I finally see this day, I decided to take one of my worse possibility."

"fuck!! One of the worse?? ending a life is the worst decision ever.."

"no!! there are worse things that can still happen to me.."

"I know..rather I understand you thiru, maybe that's why I like you so much. Every teenage girl dreams to have a bad ass boyfriend. whom only she can nurse back."

"the hurt puppy yeah??only thing I am a stray dog. well if things don't go well from now..if I still don't get a freaking piece of paper!! then life is basically an end for me. the society in which we live in sucks. they say that every teenager's turn bad because their parents weren't strict enough. but they never think the other effects that happen to their kids who once asked a million questions about moon and the stars.." I said and walked near a concrete sit out near the corner of my school.

"miss talking to your dad??miss being the one you were with your parents??

"not quite!! I look at my dad now and think is he the same person to whom I looked upto??" he didn't even care about what I was going through. Every one plays the tough dad role here. but in the process they forget to love them as well."

"the society.. I stopped caring about what people say about me. but that doesn't mean that it doesn't hurt me!! It's just that I have got numb from the pain. but leave it na its not the right time to talk about that." I could see the way her eyes shrank and her skin grew pale as she said those words.

"you don't have to say it to me or anyone. and thanks for everything you did so far!! I will never forget about it." I said and started walking to the parking lot.

"no!!! Forget about it… its better that way!! Don't think things like this."

"ok I will try!!!" she gave me a look which knew that I won't forget it even for a second of my life. There is nothing more, scary in the world then to know that you are more than capable of hurting the ones you love. I felt like killing myself not because I didn't appreciate the value of life or I was too scared to face my family. I wanted to take my own life because for me that was the only option. Maybe, every suicidal person thinks the same way. but ending ones life is never an option, it is a choice forced to take. It is forced onto to others by the hypocritical society which is unforgiving and brutal. Maybe it's a choice the educational institutes like my schools forces on many more like me. I was at my most vulnerable stage, I didn't have anywhere to go. I lost all my parental support, I was not thinking straight and completely stressed out. As I said suicied is never an option, it is always a choice forced on others. I don't know what made me so different than others. I don't know how I had amrita beside me to not only pull me back from the dead, but also helped me to pull myself together. But I do know one thing, many others are not as lucky as me to have someone to pull them back.

"I am not all ready to give you the hall ticket!! But just because your father said that you will get mentally affected and also because your uncle has earned a name for himself, I am forced to give it to you. We where expecting 100 % pass this year. do you know what that means??" princi asked me with a disgusting look, in his eyes I was a pig in a gutter covered with human sick. I didn't answer his question, because he didn't want me to answer anything. It was his soul right to treat me like a cheap whore picked up from the darkest alley's of Mumbai. He vent out his anger on me and made me to kneel down while he did so. "you have to write exams for math and physics!! Write one tomorrow and another the following day." he tells with a cracking old voice. I was less then a week away from "the boards". "sir I will write both the exams tomorrow itself."

"are you sure you can pass??you didn't clear any math exam for the past two years!! What makes you think you can pass in the boards?? You are like my child thiru!! You can't handle the shame when everyone asks about your percentage after the results are out. How can you face your relatives and friends?? I can't even imagine the amount of shame your dad, a highly influential man will be put through." there was a long pause after he tried to sound caring. My princi was a very good con man indeed, if my princi said such words like 'he is my child!! I want him to have a bright future.' most of the parents melt. The funny part is that only the student knows in which part of the body he will have a bright future.

"sir I am confident that I can pass!!"

"but I am not!! Children these days are very selfish, you don't even think about how your parent's feel. see imagine this. If you fail, which you will! Your parents can't face anyone. Even when going to a relatives house, supermarket, or any other functions. You will be the topic of the hour. And your parents will be in disgrace. but if you directly write the supplementary and score well and maybe even get a medical seat. Think how proud your father will feel."

"I want my hall ticket……………sir and I am going to write the boards and pass in it as well."

"so naïve of you. you are worth nothing in life!! You can just get hit by a truck and die. At least you won't cause permanent pain to others."

"sir…….for people like me death is a gift……..for people like me!! We are cursed to live everyday."

After my filmsy dialogue a series of cane strikes followed, which was really not a big thing to me at all. I was expecting it to be like that. Well so much for someone to say that he was like my dad. he actually wanted me dead just because his school will get a good business after recording the highest pass percentage. I wish he had just said it out of anger, but he meant each and every word he said.

Where the line ends

"as I said I am forced to give you the hall ticket. you have to write both the exams tomorrow. And try to pass it!! Even if I do give you the hall ticket, I have my ways of taking it back!" he said and ordered me to go out. "what the fuck did he just say??" I swear I heard a threat in his voice.. the way his wrinkled forehead formed a sharp V shape and his face turning red was a sight not a pretty sight to see.

"so did you get the hall ticket??" asif asked over the phone

"no bro I have to write two more exams……."

"ook ook…come to our PS3 joint"

"I think what I said was a bit subtle to you!!! I need to write fucking two more exams in less than 5 days of the boards."

"I heard!! Just get your ass over here!!"

"here I am bro!! now what the hell are we going to do??" I was screaming at asif, who could barely hear my voice. The entire joint was filled with hardcore game freaks, who liked to keep the volume up all the time. The PS3 joint was set up in a residential area. And the complaints about the noise level was literally unheard of. "catch it." bharat said, and threw me a wireless joystick. "I heard he called you in again. What did he say? Did he give you the hall ticket?" even in the chaotic place, I could somehow clearly hear him. "he tried to brainwash me, and he tried to brainwash me and also he tried to threaten me." I said and selected my player, I always used to play with kofi Kingston. "it always happens bro! but relax man. They will give it to you." asif screamed from behind and handed me a bottle of coke, Which I refused. "then what about me? I should just sit in that hell hole till june and write the supplementary exam?" bharat looked back at him, and snatched the coke from his hands. Asif was completely taken aback from his question. He didn't know how to react and pretended that he didn't hear bharat at all.

"well everybody enjoyed themselves right?? And try to forget what happened today. And be relaxed. You guys will get the hall ticket" asif was telling us, and kick started his bike. "got a call dude!" bharat told him and pointed toward his denim jeans pocket. The name central jail flashed on the screen. Bharat forcefully switched on the loudspeaker. "hello. Is this asif's father? Sir tell your son to come to the school immediately, along with his hall ticket. We have given him the hall ticket by mistake." We stood in shock as we heard the voice of an old woman over the phone. Asif's face turned pale when he heard this. "I am in a meeting now. I will tell him to come." asif replied her, with his base voice and tried to sound elderly. "this whole fucking thing is designed in a way that we won't get through!!! Even a deaf person, with a hearing aid could clearly make it out that the person that replied her with a base voice didn't even hit puberty." bharat said looking at asif and took a sip of coke. asif looked at his phone for a minute or so, and put the number on reject list, and swore of never going near the central jail again. Bharat eyes were filled with despair and certainly the mix of pepsi with cocaine didn't help the way he looked. His already small eyes, were seeming to get sucked into his eye socket and was on a trajectory to enter his brains. "nobody is that lucky!" he commented and continued to fill up the bottle of pepsi with another packet of cocaine. "stop taking it man. Otherwise you will end up in doing things you will regret." I continued to speed away across many heavy duty vehicles. "bro don't think I am taking under the influence of coke! Just hit a god damn truck man, lets end this." He said pointing at a truck containing some constructional bricks. "here take it man! Drink this it gives you the courage to do it." he said and kept the bottle of pepsi in front of my face. I guess that's the beauty of alcohol and drugs, one will never realize what a complete asshole they are. Until it is too late. "I am just kidding hero! You really think I will kill myself??" he said and tried to sound funny.

"are you ready to write the exam ra nana??" naidu sir asked me by seeing from the top of his reading glasses.

"yes sir."

"don't think I will pass you unless you write well."

"I know" I tried not to make eye

"hmm child if you want you can revise for sometime, ask sir for permission" akhil sir said with his cracking voice, akhil was a math lecturer, and was the person in charge of 'teaching' us in the library.

"no I am ready to write it sir" I told naidu, who was searching the correct the key to open the drawer in his desk. After exploring each key, as if he had stolen the wooden desk with a thick glass cover. "here take it nana. Write in the physics lab." He handed over the question paper. "sir can I write it in the library?" I asked him politely, besides he always did consider me to be innocent. He didn't answer me while climbing the fleet of stairs. But after giving me a really long stare he pointed me to go to the library. The paper was designed in such a way that I couldn't pass nor could anybody. Things were never fair in the central jail, so I decided not play fair myself. I had a chit for about 45 marks that could easily get me through it. "arrey nana even when you get so much time to read, you are hardly passing ra nana" he said and handed me the paper, He was surprised that I could pass it. "wait ra nana! I think it is better if you write the paper again." he said and asked me a few theory question and made me do some derivation in front of him. I did as he said. "you can go now! Show your paper to princi sir".

"hi!! I just finished my physics re-re-re-re-re exam, will be writing math soon" I texted amrita and laid back against the concrete sit out near the hell whole. 'great even she is busy now! No where to go now.' I thought to myself and was going through the list of some never ending formulae. I thought of meeting bharat, but the last time I went near his house, his mom was screaming at me to enter his house and talk. I had to jump out of his back yard to avoid any conversation with her. The whole thing hit bharat really hard, asif had told me earlier that he had quit eating and didn't have anything in his system except for whisky and cocaine along with many liters of carbonated drinks. Although I had a gap of two hours to write another exam, I preferred not to go home or pick any calls.

"here take the paper and go write in the library, akhil told me. Me and asif were close to akhil sir, he used to smoke in the same tea shop. Where asif and bharat used to do buy many packets of cigar. The math exam was very well done with the help of my chits. I was extremely cautious while doing it, as If I got caught. Then the whole thing was going to go down the drain.

"hello sir, Good evening. Haa yes sir. He is here" our librarian was speaking over the phone, While I completed my last 10 mark question and hid my chit inside my shirt. "yes sir! He is writing the second paper!! Ok I will check him now" the librarian got off the phone and went through my paper, to find any sort of chit and checked my pockets for an electrical gadgets. "be happy you are going to get your hall ticket today, go to the princi's chamber at 4.00 exactly." "didn't even sleep properly for over two days sir. I will be there before 4.00 itself." I told him and tied my supplementary sheets to the main booklet. I really didn't want to address anybody as 'sir'. I rushed down the fleet of stairs, I was waiting down near the princi's chamber.

"hey come here! The princi had some personal work, he is not here now. Come tomorrow." the lady sitting inside the reception told me after getting hanging up on the landline. I was sure that she hated me. "oh! Is it so…..mam? well the princi told me to take the hall ticket today itself! So if you can ask him about it, I will appreciate it". "no come tomorrow!!" she replied, rather barked at me. "if you are in such a hurry wait till suresh sir comes. Your hall ticket is in his office" she said and received another call again. The strange thing about this was, she wasn't involved in any conversation. Rather she was talking on phone, like teen girls do when they are on hone with their boyfriend while their parents are watching them. "still waiting here??" she asked me, covering the receiver with her hand. "it is raining out. So yeah I will wait here." I said and started texting on my phone. I didn't get any text back from amrita, I buried myself in the steel chair and was enjoying the rain outside. The rain was certainly refreshing, the smell of wet mud was intoxicating. I removed my glasses and kept both my palms on my eyes, the feeling was just soothing. Also this was the first time that I had noticed, that there was a small piece of fiber glass broken from the top left edge of my left lense. "pheeeew!! The girl surely has a strong slap." I thought to myself and kept my hands on my cheeks. "what is he doing here?? You wrote the exams??" CEO screamed at me, as he entered into the main reception. "all done sir. I am just waiting for the hall ticket" I got up from the chair from adjusted my specs. "the princi has gone out now, come back tomorrow!!" he said, walking towards his office. "sir! Mam said that my hall ticket was in your office" I said looking at the receptionist. After passing a disgusting look to her. He went towards his office and said. "oooh hoooo I left my office keys in my tuition center." he said with an awkward smile and commanded on of our peons to get it. "go in cycle after the rain stops." he tells, and walks into the staff room. "hey go now!! Come tomorrow, I have never seen anyone talk to sir with such disrespect." the receptionist yelled from inside the glass box.

"what is the hurry mam? The rain will stop soon" actual fact was, the rain was getting heavier by the minute.

"are you a fool? Just go now? You don't understand what I am trying to say?"

"I really do!! Considering that princi's car is just standing outside."

"what??? What did you just say??"

"you heard me." I said and headed to the parking lot. To my surprise I saw amrita's non geared bike parked right next to mine. I brushed my hands over the seat and was thinking of texting her. "uuuh god damn!! Still no reply." I thought it would be better if I would meet up with bharat and get to know how he is held up. And as expected he didn't call me back or replied to my texts. "now that explains the situation". I thought to myself and ride into the rain.

It was 11.00 am and the sun was still hiding behind a cover of thick black clouds. And I was sitting in front the princi's chamber yet again and was waiting for the hall ticket. "all of this for a piece of paper" I was beginning to like the way I saw speaking to myself, it was like an insane me asking a more insane me for solutions.

"hey come here. The princi is…………"

"not here and most probably attending a very important meeting with another board member. And I have to come again tomorrow?" I asked her with a sarcastic smile.

"yes! Come back tomorrow at 11.00. you can go now!"

"ooh I understand mam. I am sure that if I go inside the princi's chamber I won't find him there. I don't mind staying here for the night also because I just have three days to prepare for my board exams. And if I don't get it today! And I end up telling my dad and my uncle about the entire story and I do something which I may regret……..Then it will be a huge problem for your prestigious educational institute." I tried to sound as though I had some leverage, but the actual fact was that I was harmless like a pug.

"go and talk to suresh sir." She said and didn't bother my presence thereafter.

"sir may I come in?" I asked CEO, who was relaxing back on the beige coloured sofa. "did you finish both the exams?? How much did you get in math?" "I don't know sir, the paper is not yet corrected." "then how did you expect to get the hall ticket uh? Hey call akhil." he commanded another peon. After a minute or so, akhil reached down with my paper. "sir he has passed sir." he said and handed my paper to the CEO. After another scan through my paper and having a cup of tea, and some pan and speaking with princi over the phone. He finally told the receptionist to give me the hall ticket. MY HALL TICKET, a freaking piece of paper.

That ruined my life by serving as a leverage to people like my CEO, who forgets the office keys. "I am surprised you got the hall ticket thiru." Akhil sir told me, while leaving the CEO's office. "why sir? I am not that dull! At least I don't think so." I told him and extended my hand out. "no no you are not dull. It is just that we made you think that you are dull. there is a lot you don't know about this place." he said and shook my hand. "tell me sir!! I was never supposed to get this paper right?" I asked him pointing towards the paper. "no child you and many people were not supposed to get it. Many students stopped attending classes after second pre board. Suresh sir was able to convince them that they were useless. But you and your friend are too adamant." he said While going down to the parking lot. "me and asif are not easy to influence sir!" "no not asif. You and bharat! Asif Is a child of power and privilege, did you notice that whenever you people get punished. Asif never gets those red marks on his hands?" "sir now its too obvious, but why are you telling me now?" I asked in curiosity. "in short child, your entire second pre board was fixed." "you still didn't answer me sir. And how can anyone fix an exam whose attendance is compulsory?" "everyone writes the exam, but we don't correct all the papers, we only correct the papers of the students in the library. And you know about the checking process. Don't think cheap about us child, we have to do it, suresh sir and princi keeps our original certificates with them and closes our mouths with cash." He said and stood near the house of pain. "so all the hard work was for a waste?" I was shocked by what I was hearing. The whole fucking thing was a scandal. and the students, whose parents believe that these institutions mould there children into a successful human being. Were being used as pawn. "yes thiru! I can't take the way suresh and princi play mind games with the every parents. Every parent that steps inside the princi's chamber. Will be convinced that there child is on a bad track, they never believe you people! Some even gave us permission to hit the students and teach them." akhil said and was continuously surveying the area. "sir!!! I feel like a looser now!, why are you telling me this now?" I asked him with a wide smile on my face, although I was supposed to be in shock. I felt like laughing my heart out, I was laughing so much that my stomach hurts. "suresh sir is going to remove me from this PU college. I am thinking of teaching in some university now. Don't tell anyone that I told you this, even if you say. No one will believe you." He said with a cunning smile and extended his hand again. "sir, I am thinking about writing a book on my life here sir. Maybe I will write about what you told me." the smile on my face grew only wider. "oh you want to be a writer? First............ pass your board exams." He said and wished me luck. I walked across the 'house of pain'. many of the people who were tortured there still hadn't got the hall tickets. I kick started my bike and accelerated to hear the sound of bike, echo across the empty parking lot for the last time. I made me way up to entrance of my school. I looked at the building, mostly made of glass in front of me. And slowed down my bike, raise my hand high and saluted it with my middle finger. I could feel the lactic acid build up in the legs, it was beginning to cramp badly. "guess that's what happens when you survive three days on whisky and a six pack beer can." I thought to myself and speed away to bharat's house.

"bro!! see what I got!!" I flashed the white with blue printed, piece of paper.

"you finally got it! Congrats man." he told me with a cheerful smile, I honestly thought he wouldn't care at all.

"and dude, I don't have any cash in my wallet. And I didn't eat any solid food in three days or so. And also I am hungry, so if you don't mind. Can I come in for lunch?"

"don't be a shy bitch idiot, well my mom refused to feed me. So let's go out for lunch." He said and quickly rushed into his room and got a bundle of 100 rupee notes and a packet of cocaine.

"thanks! A lot.. these things we do.. it means a lot to me."

The line ends

After getting three precious day to prepare for the exam I was waiting for the past two years, it arrived. Every 12th graders worst nightmare, The board exam. Bharat was a statistic student and had a day less to prepare for the exams. Bharat had got his hall ticket a day after me. And the way he got it was practically inhumane.

"how was the exam bro??" I asked him over the phone.

"I was nervous like hell, in the starting. But as I started to answer the paper, I was more comfortable."

"ok cool. So you got any question from the model papers? our school gave us a guarantee, that majority of the questions will be asked from the models itself?" I asked him with such curiosity, like a puppy waiting for its master to return home quickly to feed him, when he is hungry.

"no bhai! Not even one. Everything is from the textbook. study it no matter what. All these days of torture went for a fucking waste" he continued.

"not exactly. Will fill you in afterwards."

"whatever go study! And don't let those days go for a waste man." he said and hung up, you could clearly make out the pain in his voice.

The first exam was filled with formalities, with three invigilators in a room, and all of them looked sadistic or depressive. The way the chief invigilator does things made me think that he has classics obsessive compulsive disorder tendency. The first exam was a walk in the park for me, it was biology. The second was physics. And as I expected nothing from the model question paper had turned up, I got I tip from my tutor, about the questions displayed on PUE website. And they had higher possibilities of turning up, and they did. The first thing I did after getting the question paper, was to check if I could write something. And instigate the worst possible scenario and later on assure myself that I could clear the exam. The math exam was also a big hurdle that I crossed with some major night studies with asif and solving the 'ZEN' model paper, from which all physics, chem, math and bio had turned up. And chemistry was the last hurdle to cross. After chem, we had five days of preparation for the languages. Maybe it was luck that the day my main subjects had been done with, was the day india celebrated as 'HOLI' the festival of colours.

"ok bhai! All done come near lovers spot at 1.00 sharp." Asif said and dropped me off at my place. "all cool man, I'll just dress up and get my ride." I said while strangers, majority were under influence of alcohol or 'bang' a local alcoholic drink, applied colours on me. I left home early, almost as soon as asif left. I had a plan, Before I went to the lover's spot.

I wanted to meet amrita. And I took a de-tour and crossed by her place. There I saw her, with blue denims and a white tops. And her face completely covered in pink. I parked my bike, while many strangers surrounded me and applied colours and few even danced in front of me, whereas a few made me dance with them. "hi!! Happy holi" I told her and applied a shiny orange colour on her cheeks. "happy holi!!!!!" she said and dumped a huge load of red colour on my head. "what are you doing here??" she asked me while wiping the colours near her eyes and forehead. "just going to play holi with my friends near by, so I thought of seeing you. Been a long time yeah!!!" I said wiped my glasses. "ooh god thiru! You are going to play now? I barely even recognize you." She said and a smile appeared on her face. I don't blame her for that, every human in town were applying colours on each other, even while driving. A few children targeted vehicles to ambush with their water balloons and eggs. "looking that bad eh?" "yes!! Come inside and wash your face, she said and grabbed my hand and started pulling me inside her house. "hey no wait up! What should I tell your parents then?" I tried to stop her. "you think I am insane? Why will I even bring you inside my house. If my parents weren't out?" she said and went inside her room, I followed her. All I could hope was that some nosy neighbor won't complain to anyone of my presence in her house. She went near the dressing table in the side of her king size bed. And started wiping her face with a towel. "I always watch the rain from this window here!" she said and pointed towards an old window frame, with its bottom edges swollen. "I get a great view of the pond there." She stood in front of me and stared dusting off her clothes. "let me help you." I said and ran my hands across the back of her shoulder, and her neck. And I kept my hands on her waist, while I kissed the side of her neck. "what are you doing??" she asked me while closing her eyes and a smile across her lips. "not going to do anything that we both will regret." I said and kissed her ear lobe, and cheeks from the side. I was watching her from the reflection of the mirror. My hands held her waist firmly, as I continued kissing her neckline and her throat from the side. "ok that's enough" she said, suddenly opening her eyes. And pushed me back by her waist. "what are you doing thiru??" "as I said nothing that is against your consciousness, and at the moment just catching your waist." I said and was looking at her eyes, from the reflection. "oh is it so mr. waran? A part of you, is surely doing something else" she said blushing. "oh I am sorry! It's getting too much, yeah I will.... oh hell!!! I will..... leave now." I said and tried to get out fast.

"wait!! Don't panick. You look like you are seconds away from fainting."

"my heart is beating so fast that I think I'll black out!" I said and kept her hand and my chest.

"me too!!" she said and looked straight into my eyes. "don't leave thiru. Don't go now." she and moved her lips closer to mine.

Before I could react, I was catching her waist from the front and her hands was behind my head. I could feel her bubblegum tounge and her cheery lips. After a long smooch my hands were on top of her toned stomach and slowly reached her ribs just below her breasts. I could feel her warm breath, her lips were just inches away from mine. I paused for a long moment, I was looking straight into her eyes. There was not a word spoken all the while. I finally kept my hands on her breasts, that were so soft and I could feel them through the thin fabrics of her tops. After another long smooch, I lifted her tops till her neck. my hands were over her naked skin. She unbuttoned my shirt and ran her fingers over the scars on my chest and abdomen. She ran her index finger over the scar from my chest to the abdomen, it looks like a slash mark. I lifted her from near the dressing table and took her to the king size bed. I ran my fingers across her deep navel. I continued to kiss her forehead and eyes. I smooched her, kissed her neck line and followed it down her throat. I kissed her cleavage and reached her soft yet firm breasts And my hands were on both sides of her. The denim's were off soon. I ran my finger, across her legs and kissed her thighs. I was in between her and we were looking deep into each other's eyes, I could see her breasts move up and down as I increased my speed. There was dead silence not a word was spoken in between us during the whole time, except for some loud pitbull music that was being played way across the street. I didn't smile at her, but her eye's did the smiling for her. She crossed her long longs on back, locking me in the position. I could feel her breasts move faster, as I increased my pace. She closed her eyes as I began to kiss her lips.

"so many scars on your body!" she said with her sweet voice, she was laying beside me in a quilt. This was the first sentence spoken in a long time.

"yeah.. behind every scar there is a story!!" I said and wrapped her around from the side.

"most of it is from your stupid races? and show off stunts na??" her fingers were running over the scar on my chest.

"equal – equal, 50 % races and 50 % by the artists"

"those animals hit you badly!!" she said while placing her lips on the scars on my shoulder.

"don't talk about that now! Today is the best day of my life!" I said and kissed her eyes and cheek. The feeling can not be expressed in words.

"is it so mr. waran?" she said with her husky voice and removed the bed spread from me. "heyy wait!!! I am totally naked." I jumped out of the bed and almost slipped on to the floor, to get my jeans.

"well miss. Rai. You are going to get some payback!" I said and tried to remove the bed spread that covered her naked body. She was clutching on to it, after a pause I removed it of her forcefully.

"this is not fair yar!!" she picked up her denims and rushed to the washroom.

"what's not fair? Now that's equal!!" I said and watched her rush to the washroom. she returned after a few minutes with the same white tank top and blue denims.

"I am sorry. For what happened that day.. and thanks for coming back! I really didn't think that you will come back…. Rather I hoped that you won't come back.."

"your really thought that I will let you die?? You were serious in that stupid decision…. I could see that in your eyes. Everyone has a tough time in their life. And during those times, people tend to make stupid choices! But remember I am the one that pulled you back from taking the worst decision ever!!" she said keeping her head down and caught my hand.

"there is no way in hell that I will forget that day…….. there is no way in the darkest day in hell that I will forget what you did for me…" I said and hugged her tight.

"its getting late now! My parents will come any minutes. Go out fast." she said and pushed me out of the bed. "this place is a mess! Let me help you." I said and picked up the quilt that was on the floor. "go now thiru! I will clean it up and take a shower." she said and hugged me. "ok will miss you!!" I said and kissed her. "hmmm ok." She said and adjusted her hair. "hmm ok?? I will really miss you!…… You!!!" I said and hugged her tight. "that's funny. I know a few men that have told me the same thing just to get me in bed, but you are the only one to tell me that after you get out of bed." she said and placed her hands on both sides of her hips. "does it hurt to know?? To know that I have………?" she asked looking straight into my eyes. "I don't know." "hmm thought so…." She said with her disappointed eyes. I placed my finger on her lips. "I don't know what I have done to earn so much of your trust. Well it does hurt me to know! But you did what you had to do, no did to explain yourself to me or to anyone. I am alive because of you. Nobody has done so much to me, till now." I said and rubbed her cheeks. "ok go!! Goo!! Go now!! I will call you in the evening." she said and rushed me out. "holy shit!! Its 1.30 now." I was going through the list of texts that I had received along with the seven missed calls.

"Look who has finally decided to show us his esteem presence!!" bharat told asif, and threw me a can of beer, both of them were hardly recognizable. Their face was covered with orange colour and a straight vertical line of red from their foreheads to their nose. "so bro? got stuck in traffic??" asif questioned me in a sarcastic way. "yeah man!! You did not see the traffic near amrita's house? We could even see waran's bike there" bharat commented and took a long sip of beer. "dude her house was nearby!! So it was natural for me to go see her, I mean it has been a long time since I have spoken to her." I said and watch the slight foam of beer gush out of the tin. "unbelievable!!! So you actually did go to her house!!! I cant believe you fell for it!!" asif was laughing uncontrollably. "even you are a prey to the great bharat!!!" he continued. "haaa ook I fell for it man! It was a good prank and I am really embarrassed." I told them mockingly, and tried not to smile. "the only way you could have fallen for it is….." bharat paused and didn't bother to complete saying the sentence. "is if you were…" asif commented and started moving his hips to and fro. "fuck you bro!! ooh I wish that happened." Bharat looked at me from the corner of his eye and said "we have seen you for two years so drop the annoying act." and burst out laughing. the rest of the gang arrived in 15 minutes interval and all of them were really. "how could they even drive." Was the question of the moment. This was the first time, I enjoyed myself in hubli. The little drizzle that occurred occasionally because of humidity was soothing. As the day came to end with taking a shower in the middle if street, which reminds me of 'rain disco' a popular theme park game. Their were many people dancing in it and few began to pass out on the street. I had realized that everything is ephemeral And everything always has an end. "arreyyyyy bhai tho bhi wapas janai wala hai salai (even you are going to go back home soon brother)" bharat mumbled and passed out on the street.

When the line ends 2

We had about five days of study vacation for the languages. I spent most of those days in the PS3 joint. And went on long rides with my friends without having a fixed destination. The rest of the exams went by within a blink of an eye. As I was writing the last few sentences of the final question of the last exam, I was looking at the bruises on my knuckles. The bruises had slowly started to heal. Maybe it was too dramatic, but I wanted to see CEO again and say the words "f u c k o f f" on his face, loud and clear. I could hear the final bell echo through the place. And the silent exam hall, had a carnival atmosphere. "thanks for the help! What's your name??" I asked the girl, that was sitting beside me. She did tell her name, but I couldn't hear it in the commotion outside. I just smiled and pretended that I heard her "well then!! I will never see you again." I could see a wide smile come across her face. As soon as I left the exam hall, I felt like I had been awakened from a long period of cryogenic sleep. The entire atmosphere was spectacular. I could see people taking selfies and updating their facebook profile, few others were taking pictures with their friends, while some rushed to get a last look of their crush. It had the right mix of happiness, relief and sadness all at once.

I started to make my way down the crowded staircase, the entire place was festive, if none the less. I had made my way down a floor, inch by inch. I finally saw her again, her eyes were partially closed as the mid day sun hit her face, her face glistened of sweat and appeared to shine. She was chatting with a group of friends, the same group that always tried to put her down. She covered her phone with her hands and began to dial a number. She adjusted her hairs, behind her ears and waited patiently for the answer. The phone in my pocket began to vibrate. I didn't pick her call. Rather I didn't even realize that she was the one that called me, till much later. She threw her phone inside the handbag in disappointment and wiped her forehead covered in sweat. I was staring at her from the opposite side side of the floor, we were standing on parallel side of the corridor. She did make an eye contact with me, and waved her hand from side to side. But I just stood there, and was looking at her face. I was mesmerized. My phone began to vibrate again, 'amy calling' flashed on the mobile screen. I was forced to pick the call up, as I could sense a pinch of anger building on her face.

"how was your exams?" I asked her over the phone, and was looking right at her, across the parallel corridor.

"it was ok!! And what has happened to you?" I was slowly getting hypnotized by her voice, I never really liked to talk over phone much, but just her voice had a hypnotic effect on me.

"just watching the left cheek of the most beautiful girl I've ever seen in my life! It's glistening in sweat."

"hmmmm.. your lines seem a little too rehearsed!!" the smile on her lips grew wider, she wiped the sweat of her cheeks. With her slender long finger.

"maybe it is!! But it seems to make sense only when I say it to you."

"whatever!! pick me up at lovers spot around 4.00 ok? I have to go now! And thiru, no drinking too much, no over speeding or racing and no stunts!" her eyes grew wider, as she said the last few lines.

I made my way out of the examination centre, I could see asif chatting with his bunch of fan following girls, nashi was on phone, as always and bharat was trying to do a burnout on virat's bike. "good to see that you got your bike back!!" I said while reaching my fist up for a knuckle up. "hey man!! Long time! After your beating that day I was sure, that you were going to kill shekar." "can't deny that I wanted to or I can still do it now. But bhai he is not worth it." "I can't believe that I heard that from you!! what has happened to you man?" he asked surprised at my answer, I bet he was waiting for some abusive words. "real question is what happened to you??you got the ride back!!" I asked him and switched his ride's engine off, while bharat was still trying the burnout. "leave it! Don't make me think about it." "all the best for NDA man! Cheers I will never see you again!" virat soon took his bike from bharat, who finally learnt the art of standing burnouts. "fucker everything has finally ended man!!" asif said, while taking some selfies with the remaining girls of his fan following. "lets go talk about it in the yoga center." bharat dragged us to the parking lot, and we had yet another friendly race till the PS3 joint, bharat always called it as our yoga center. Somehow I could defeat asif in that race, "first time you ever defeated me" he said with a smirk on his face, the only reason was he let me win. "asif I have joined a CET coaching center in Bangalore, I will be going there at the end of the month" bharat told asif, how was trying to get the briefcase, in the money in the bank ladder match. "really bro! I helped him in paying the fee's and all the formalities, bharat is going to stay with me till the CET exams." I said while I pushed asif, from the top of the ladder. "hey bloody fuckers! You didn't even till me that!." He said and paused the game. "just for a month bro! I will be back in hubli soon." bharat said and resumed the game. "hey waran!! We are going to attend a small party okay? Our kind of party....... Tomorrow at 6.00 in the evening." asif said and hit me with a steel chair. "about that!! I am leaving tomorrow in the morning at 6.00 am" I uttered out, bharat and asif together tapped on the pause button and started the abusive marathon. I was surprised that humans could abuse that long without a break. "dude I need to attend some family function!!" I told them with my helpless eyes. "dude go in the middle of the street, undo your pants and start fucking yourself with your bikes silencer." Asif was fuming with anger. "what ever asshole. you won't come back to hubli! I know that!! But you could stay a little long at least! Bewada saala.(alcoholic)"

"I never really thought that this day would come, and I am having everything I want with me now!" I said and handed my helmet to amrita, who was sitting behind me. "your hair looks great no matter what! So please put it on" I persuaded her to wear it. "then what about you??" she asked me and wrapped her hands over my shoulder and rested her palms on my chest. "me?? it doesn't matter what happens to me!........ I mean uh…. I've got used to driving like this." I accelerated into a narrow street, that was a short cut to my friends PG. "why are you breaking so frequently?" she asked me curiously and adjusted herself. "well just like that!" I said and applied the front disk brakes. Which made her whole body come in contact with my back. "oh this is why? You pervert! Is this better?" she said and hugged me from the back. "now that's way better." the whole journey of an hour, seemed to go like minutes. Every next gear I hit was an inner conflict between the my heart and my brain, my heart was verbally abusing my mind for directing my legs to change gears. Her palms were over my chest, the side of her cheek was on my back and I would feel her warm breath. I wasn't sure if she had a smile on her face, but I visualized her to have it and just that thought made me smile too.

"why couldn't we just go to some restaurant, that has some great food and the acoustics of some romantic numbers that reflect around the entire place??" I asked her while making ourselves comfortable in the room.

"we could have! But that won't be as special as being with you alone…" her eyes lit up and kept her hands over my bruised knuckles.

"yuups! This is so much better than sitting parallel to each other in a crowded restaurant with people looking at us in every move we make." I said and hugged her from the side.

"hmmmm does every guy drink beer or what??" she asked me pointing at the empty bottles in the left corner of the room.

"nope!!! But most guys from v.n.c do!!" I said as she rapped herself around me.

"don't talk about that place now!!!" her husky sweet voice turned stern. "A beautiful girl is sitting right next to you… and you still think about that place?" her husky cheerful voice returned.

"not just any beautiful girl!! The girl who is the persona of the word beautiful and not just sitting right next to me" I said and caught the side of her hip.

"Is it so mr. waran?? Or is it a line to get me in bed??" her giggling grew louder as she wrapped her hands around my shoulder.

"ohhh!!! Well…. If I wanted that….. I am not saying that I don't want it!!! But if I was that desperate to get in bed with you…. Then we won't be talking right now!!!"

"well Mr. waran that day when I invited you inside my house and let you in my room. It was for you to wash your face and have a nice cup of coffee which you would make….. but we certainly did end up doing something else……." her sparkling eyes met mine and the lips on her face grew wide.

"ooh miss. Rai! I tried to control myself…. I did control myself … but the physiological effect was bound to happen."

There was a smile on her face. But I could the guilt in me which was rushing in. "regrets?? Any regrets about what we did??" my eyes failed to meet hers.

"Idiot!! Then why do you think I am with you now??" she kept her slender fingers on my chin and brushed her soft lips with mine. Our tounges fought with each other, as I pushed her gently on the single cot bed. My hands were on her hips as I slowly kept my hand on her bare toned stomach and made my way till I could feel her ribs.. I looked at her eyes that was filled with confusion.

"not going to do anything which we will regret...... and this time I mean it" I told her and kissed the side of her neck and forced myself to get up from the bed.

"hmmm sorry!!!....... come here na!" she said stretching her hands wide still laying on the bed. I laid back as she kept her head on my arm and her hands across my chest.

"don't be.... I understand!! Will never do anything that will torment your consciousness." I said while looking at the ceiling fan which was rotating slowly in anti clockwise direction.

"ssshh!!!" she kept her finger on my lips and brought her lips closer to mine.

"ooooh damn it!!! How long was I out??" the only thing that woke me from my deep sleep was amrita's hands that was caressing my hair and the side of my face.

"A little over an hour...... it was such a cute sight to see you live in peace for sometime." She said and hugged me from the side. I woke up with a jolt, that was the best sleep I had in almost a month. It was slowly getting dark and I knew that it was time for her to go home. I did not want that evening to come to an end. I wanted to be stuck in it forever with my angel beside me. I tried to keep a fake smile to hide all the thoughts that was running inside me. "time for me to go?? I know don't keep that smile on your face please." Amrita noticed it, she was the only that could see through my smile. I hated her for it, I hated that I could not hide away the side of me which anyone hardly know that existed from her.

"I never really thought that a girl as beautiful as you will be with me till the end." I told her and hugged her from the side. "I used to stare at you during the school functions and be like 'is she an angel??' and try very hard to take my eyes off you!" "and yet you did nothing to get fresh with me." she said and dressed up and adjusted her hair behind her ear. "yup what can I say?? I am a gentleman!! And lets go now.. it looks like its going to rain again." I did manage to jump the traffic and get her home before dark. She didn't say anything to me during the entire travel, she was just hugging me from the back. Every time I changed into the next gear, I felt that the time I had left with her was perishing away.

"ok.. I will meet you when I get back here for the CET!! I will miss you a lot!!" I said while kissing her forehead.

"hmmm ok! Will you really miss me?? Or it is your rehearsed line for after making love?" she didn't make eye contact with me.

"what you said is insulting to say the least!! the times we spent together will always be cherished by me! Trust me… the things that happened in between us… it is not just 12th grade senior high school love.." I said catching her face with both my hands.

"yeah yeah!! Because I gave you my body? We are just eighteen and we did lot of things together!! That is all you will remember na? after a few years you will forget everything about me and hubli." she said keeping her hands on both sides of her hips.

"well the things we did together….. is just a part of my life…. the best part of my life. but the point is that, The little things which we did matters a lot to me!" I said and rubbed my palms over her cheeks.

"like what??…………… I am sorry if what I said hurts you… but You make me feel really special. And if it all was for my body.. I can't take it." this was the first time she made the eye contact during the whole conversation.

"like the first time I meet you, the times I used to stare at you in class, the day our eyes meet and you waved at me.. the care in your voice when you tell me to not do my stupid stunts, the slight anger I see in you when I still do it…." we kissed again, I did not want to let go of her. the time had come for us to depart. I slowly started to come in terms with the reality. The probability that I would see her during CET was unlikely.

"do you love me or no?? look into my eyes and say." she asked me while wrapping her hands around my neck.

"does that question really matter??" after a long hug, I saw her running towards her house. And I started my long and boring ride to my place.

Every minute of the journey back home, felt as though it was hours and hours away. It felt like a five hundred ton weight that was pulling me back. "good with you! Because I gave you my body?, we are just eighteen, you make me feel special!..... can't take it if its only for my body… I will miss you." every word she said was echoing in my empty head, I could hardly even hear the loud thunder, what made me realize about the change in weather. was the slight drizzle that hit my face. "I am nothing without her, she is just perfect!!, I am just a nobody……. she is the best thing that has ever happened to me. I will miss her with ounce of my body!! She is my special someone!! Oooh fuckkk!!! My special someone!!!! My love!!!" I thought to myself and heard the screeching sound of my bike tyres, I took a sharp turn, on any other given day the sharp turn I took would have ended by my bike getting hit by a truck. I began racing towards her again, I was cursing myself for telling D.K to tune my bike. The heavy drizzling started to pick up, and the road visibility was fucked up. "only disadvantage of wearing glasses." I thought to myself. I reached her house in a fair amount of time, but had no clue if I should meet her again or if she would want to meet me again. Would she come out or I should go in. I looked at my face on the side view mirror, my forehead was covered with my hair. My over grown beard did not make the view any better. I was completely drenched and my shirt was not tucked in, a few stains of mud were on my jeans. In short, I was looking like a terrible guy from the street that every parent will wish that will never speak to their daughters. "ooh so much for 'be the kind of guy that you want your daughter to be with'" I thought to myself. I decided to not go inside her house, as her parents would have probably got a restraining order against me, if they had seen me anywhere near her house. I parked my bike just beside the small pond, which she told that she will see a great view, every time it rained. I saw a black figure looking at my direction, I had no sure way of telling that it was amrita. I was still sitting on my ride, and was looking at the black figure that suddenly disappeared as the light went out. She came rushing out of her house in her pyjamas, with a green umbrella in her right hand. "what are you doing here you idiot!! You are completely drenched!! And oh god thiru!! You came all the way back?" she said with a shocked look and held the umbrella over my head. "I am sorry but you got to change your clothes again." I said and hugged her tight and lifted her from the ground. "I love you! I really love you!! You are the only best thing that has happened to me .... I am messed up!!, I am damaged beyond repair...... You are the only one I want to be with." I held her tight and embraced her. I didn't want to let her go even for a second. "why did you come back all the way?? Gosh thiru!! You will make me cry." She said as I could hear the sound of her laugh. "this may seem a little too melodramatic!! But I love you!! I really do!......... You saw me for a monster I was, you held my hand and brought me back from the dead!! you were there with me, when nobody would have dared to get near me. The things we did together on bed was great, it was beyond great.. it was 'awesome'. But trust me!! I love you! If this is not love!! Then I am not sure if it exists." I kissed her soft lips and sipped the rainwater that ran across her lips, the umbrella was a mile away from us. "so miss rai!! Do you love me??" I asked her, as my left knee went on the ground filled with rainwater and wet mud. "obviously you idiot!! I love you!! I looove you........" she said while I was hugging her by the waist.

Back where I belonged 2

"get up man!! It's 11.30 now, the class starts in another hour." Bharat tried to wake me up. And threatened to pour some pepsi on my face if I didn't get up soon. "no problem we will be on time!!" I said, in my cracking voice. "you sound like a 400 year old zombie, that has been awakened by a witch!!" "wow bro! you are calling yourself as a witch!!" "get up fucker!! And you skipped the part where you sound like a zombie." "agreed, between FYI zombies don't sleep for 400 years, mummies do!!" I said and got up from the bed. "too good!!! shekar will be proud of his bio student!" he said with his typical, half face smile. "uuh! Thanks for reminding me about him yet again. The day is off to a really good start." I said and was going to hit the shower. "it is noon by the way!!" he commented, "and spent the rest of the night thinking about central jail??" he asked me curiously. "yes!! Things like that don't get forgotten that easily." Before he asked me the next obvious question, "yup was thinking about her too!" I said and shut the door behind me, and hit the hot shower.

"dude can you understand what she is teaching??" bharat questioned me with a huge question mark on his face. The organic chemistry part, which the CET coacher was teaching. Remained a big mystery to us. "I don't even remember these topics man!! Did our fucking jail, even teach us this??" I replied him, and my head was being ripped in two. "dude!! If you don't feel bad, actually even if you feel bad I don't care. But the CET coaching is kinda useless!! The only reason why our school is on top of board results. Is because they hit the shit, out of us and make us mug things up. But for CET we need to apply our own brain!" I told him, which he readily agreed. "it is funny though! The last time I was in Bangalore, I was a guy who used to think on my own and do things. Now two years later, iam a cheap by heart pass type bastard." "really man! V.N.C's name is going to get fucked up when the CET results are out, the only guys that get through it will be those incredibly genius bookworms, who spent two years of life locked up in their rooms." Bharat said and after an hour and half, of trying to solve the mystery. We decided to head home early. "bro lets see if we understand anything, for a few more days. If we can't then lets just study from the study materials, nothing much we can do!" I said and kick started my bike. "going to go home this early?" I could the surprised look on his face. "you think so??"

After attending twelve classes, we decided that attending the classes were as good as not attending it. We spent the rest of the days hanging out in some the most popular places in the city. We went for go karting and I defeated him most of the time. Hung out in many different shopping centers in the city, occasionally went to a near by pub. "the view from here!! Is spectacular!! But the beer in this place is 1500 bucks plus tax." Bharat said, and clicked a few pictures of the city, covered in light drizzle and the winds were picking up fast. "it happens when you are in bar of a sky scrapper, but bro you can't beat the view from here." "don't know if its because of the beer. But building seems to touch the clouds." He said and raised his glass to the sky. "maybe that's because the owner of the drink company you are drinking is also the owner of this building." I said and bought another peg of rum. "my dad will be proud of me! He sent me so far from home, and I am wasting his cash. By drinking rum and beer in a high priced bar, filled with incredibly good looking girls." He said and started checking out some girl in a pink, party wear. "it's a shame that you have to leave back in three days. How the fuck did a month get over man? And shit dude, after CET its goodbye hubli!! I am not sure why I am saying this man, but I will miss hubli." "bhai if we studied something for a month, then we would felt the time go by, but most of the time we were hanging out in some place or the other." he said and took a sip of rum. "and you won't miss hubli.. you will just miss us and amrita….. and sorry dude, amrita is a great girl. I just heard some stories about her, and I judged her…. Fuck bro! people like me also judge??!!! But bhenchod!! You almost hit me for a girl!!" he said and jabbed me. "not just any girl!! And you deserved that man, drug addict saala." "totally agreed man. So are you really going to write a book on our miserable life in hell?" he asked as he made himself small over the extra cushioned sofa. "hmmm maybe I will. People should really get to know what is the inside story, in such reputed schools man. Maybe another thiru waran and bharat deshpande won't be born." I said and finished the glass of rum. "ooh fuck dude!! The earth can't tolerate another doppelganger of us." He said and joined her joined his hand over his head.

"so this is it man. we are leaving tonight. And then CET crap and after that its goodbye?" bharat said and packed up his suitcase. "only one thing left. Lets grab some sovenier!! And you want to drive??" I told him and threw him my bike's key. "sure man!! but…… I am not sure if I am in bangalore now. Or locked up in some mental asylum in hubli and imagining this whole thing. I mean you!! You gave me your ride's key to drive." I could hear the excitement in his voice. "the cops here are too strict on rules so drive safe." Bharat was a good driver, does everything by the book. No wonder he was always scared to sit behind me. "dude help me select a gift man. something with an umberalla on it and a card as well" I told bharat and went threw the large stacks of greeting cards. "umbrella?? Ooh you meant like this??" he pointed out at small snow globe, were a girl and guy were sitiing under an umbrella. "that is awesome brother! And pack this please." I said to the old lady in the billing counter. "I already know who it is for!!! And damn its setting in man, we were tortured, hit, bashed, smashed and we also crashed. But we were together bro….guess everything really does come to an end!!" bharat told me and we went home. "I will miss these people man, they are really friendly and the girls here are wow!!" he said while packing up the rest of his things. "still got some time left to spend in hubli also! So cheers to the happy life."

The two days of exam went faster then the speed of sound. My hopes of meeting amrita for the last time were getting megger by the minute. Asif on the other hand was delighted to see bharat, but didn't greet me at all. "anyway you will go back tonight! I am sure" he said partially closing his eyes.

"yes brother! I have too." I said and raised my hands up to guard myself. "kithe baar bola thujhe ke tum aise kaam nako kar! Tera gandmasti bhi harami (how many times have I told you to not do such things man?? fucker after today you won't come back. At least could have stayed for a day)" he was pissed at me. "haaa was waiting for it." He said as I got a call from amrita. "Go meet your girl…for the last time!! Meet your friends for the last time!!…….why are you running away from everything now??you have everything you need with you. What else do you want? Nobody can dare to question you in hubli. You have got so many contacts here that nobody can harm you. even if they tried, I will personally gut them to the ground. What is wrong with you? Just tell me fucker. What is the need to go back now?" he was furious at me and was not ready to listen to me. "it is all I wanted from the past two years man!!" I said and tried to explain myself, honestly even I did not know why I had to leave hubli so early. "whatever!!! go meet your girl… will see you in the railway station." Asif said and picked up bharat, who was kind enough to lend me his bike. I went as fast as I could, to a park near her house. There I saw her, I could see a lot of changes in her. Her curly hair had become straight, their was a thin line of mascara on her eyebrows. "hi!!!" I said and walked towards her, I always felt my heart beat faster. Whenever I was with her. Don't know if it was the anxiety but she always made my heart skip a beat. "you have become more beautiful!! Seriously too beautiful."

"hmmm is it!! I missed you.." she said and wrapped her hands on my shoulder. "why do you always wear full sleeve shirts now? I checked your fb profile. In every pic, you are either wearing a faded blue T shirt or full sleeved shirt.. Seems like you and bharat had a great time."

"naa simply… until the wounds heal completely." I said and kept my head over the side of her head. I never knew that I would be with a girl in a park and be in a romantic intimacy together.

"ummmm how was your CET??" her face was resting on my shoulder and I could feel her warm breath.

"two words…. Gang bang" I said and placed my hands on her shoulder, and was on a constant look out for the beat police.

"remember that day on the hill, when we were chatting and I dared myself to kiss you? seriously if you would have slapped me or something, I would have jumped of the hill!"

"hmmm I do" there was a smile growing on her face. "and you were so nervous, when I moved near you."

"oooh yeah I was….. actually I still am" I said and kept her hand on my chest.

"gosh!! You might get a heart attack, if your heart keeps beating like that." She said and I could see her eyes sparkle. I agree though, heart is supposed to be an invoulentery organ. I had no control over it.

"I got you something!!!" I gave her the snow globe and she unwrapped it in a hurry.

"ooh my god!! Its nice thiru.. I think I know why the umbrella was for." she said and hugged me. "read the card as well" I said and unwrapped the paper envelope.

"Those words on the card!! Its too good." Her eyes were swelling up. "Haaa let me the read the bottom lines which I wrote for you, it is kinda lame. But anyways.... 'this may very well be the last time I will ever see you, but I do want to tell you a few things before I go away from my light, that found me when I was rotting away in the dark. The first time I ever saw you, my heart started to beat faster... I felt like I would blackout....maybe it is the last time I am seeing you, but even now as I write these words, my heart still does skip a beat. You are the persona of the word beautiful, I may not believe in life, above the heavens. But if you ever asked me, I would say that you are the sole survivor from the heavens above. There are a lot of things that come to my mind, when I think about you. But I never got a chance to thank you for slapping some sense to me that day, between your slap still does sting when I think about it. Even though I hate to drink tea, the cup of elachi tea we had in the slight drizzles always makes my taste bud want more of it. I still wish I could freeze time, and be with you for eternity, that place will be called my paradise.' Hmmm I kinda wrote that in 5 mins, so sorry if it was lame!" I said and handed over the blue card with white designs in the corner. "That was the best thing anybody said to me..." she said and hugged me tight, all I could do was to embrace and savour each and every second of it. "Hey!!this is not the last time that you are going to see me!!! Can't you just ask me? Or are you going to make me wait forever??" I could sense some cracking in her voice, there was eagerness in her voice. I didn't want to let her go. "Don't go.. Stay with me here, you tell me that I am that best thing that has happened to you. But did you even bother to ask me how I felt? How I felt about you? You are different from the people here, the only guy that was good to me. You are the only guy, that I can surely say that loved me more then you loved my body." I could feel some tears roll down her cheeks and onto my shirt. I didn't know what I should say or do. "The last time when you dropped me home. All I could think about was you, I was even standing in front of window, some part of me hoping that you will comeback again. And you did. That meant a lot to me." she said while we were in our tight embrace. "sometimes I feel that you don't deserve me. Sometime's I feel lucky that you are with me now. You deserve a very happy life. I have to let you go!! You deserve A kind off life with full of sunshine and rainbows, whereas me...... I am just a dark cloud on your sunny day. And I shall always remain like that. I am not the prince charming that you deserve. I am the shink in the armour, I am just nothing but broken pieces of who I was....... I am nothing!" I kept my hands around her waist. "Don't you dare say that again!! I was hoping that you will ask me something else not this!!" She said and pushed me away from her. "No matter how little you feel about yourself. I know that you're a great guy, that every girl will wish to have." I could see her face that was a mess, but she still looked as beautiful as ever. Even with her cheeks puffed up and her nose red. "I will stay.. it doesn't matter where I go! I am just incomplete without you. But if I do.. things will never be the same." I am not exactly sure why I said that, deep inside me I always wanted to stay with her. She had a blank face, with a faint smile on it. "Pick up your call.." she said and took out my phone, from my right jean pocket. Dad calling flashed on the screen. "Here speak na!! she tapped on the receive botton and kept the phone on my hear. "Hello..... Uhh I hope your CET went well, get home early. We are done with the packing." My dad said over the phone. "Ok. will be there" I replied and quickly disconnected the call. "So finally speaking to your dad." she said and kept her hands behind my neck. "Well not really but getting there." "I don't know why I asked you to stay. If you end up staying here by any chance. It will be like killing you with the same hands that saved you once. But that doesn't mean that we have to end na??" She asked me curiously, her eyes started to build fear. And separated herself from me. "Some more time please..." I hugged her again. "Ok.. But you got to get home early. And when does your train leave?" "late night why??." "ooh.... That means its going to leave early..... What time??" "In about an hour and half" I said and cursed myself for telling her that.

"Do not say it.. I can see it in your eyes! Just please don't do it to me." she said and did not let go off me. "Just some seconds more please. I will never see you again I promise." I said and crushed her with my arms.. "What did you just say to me??" She was furious and her hard right hand made an impression on my face.. "I am letting you go!! There is no other way this ends. I let you go!!" I said and kept both my hands on her cheeks and kissed her strawberry lips. "You idiot! I love you so much!! I knew it that you were going to do this! I just knew it! Why are you doing this to youself? Its alright if you don't want to construct your future based on me... But you won't last a day without me!" Her face was filled with disgust, tears rolling down her cheeks. I couldn't tell her a single word. I had a faint smile on my face and tears escaped from my right eye more then my left. "Noo!! Not about you!! This one is on my hands... I got to let you go!! I love you!!" I whispered in her ears. "Ooh god!! You are thinking of it again na? you want to end your life again!!! I won't let you asshole." She said and began to slap me with both her hands continuously. "I won't!!! Look at me!!!! I will never even think of such things again. The life which I live is the one you have given me.. I will live everyday and appreciate it." I told her looking dead straight into her bloodshot tear filled eye. I caught hold of her hands and watched her sob. She buried her face on my chest and her long tails cut through my skin. "Shhh I know!! I know why you are doing this.... I know." She kept repeating the same sentence. I Kept both my hands on her waist, Parted her lips with mine and our tounge's met for one last time. I don't remember how long it went on for. All I could remember was her pushing me off her with her tear filled eye, I was cursing myself of having put her though it.. "I will miss you!" I think she said those words. I could barely hear her voice and make a sensible sentence out of it. "Don't look back Waran!!" that was the last sentence my Angel ever said to me. I kick started my bike, it took me three tries. I could feel my leg going numb. I watched her face disappear slowly as I went further away from her. The sickening feeling in my stomach returned.

"Bhai. Thank for the bike." I said and threw Bharat his bike's key. "what happened man? let me drop you, you look like crap. I fucking knew that you were going to do something

like this!! Do you want it?? It will make you feel better.....
for now"

"No!! All coke did to me was to make me feel better, when
the actual reality was that it screwed up my life pretty well.
And bhai!!! she went away man...... Forever. I will never see
the face of the girl, because of whom I am alive today!" I
think a few drops of tears escaped my eyes.

"What the hell did I just hear?? Go back to her broo!!! You
literally can't survive a day without her. This ain't some love
drama shit! You can't live without her!!" Bharat shook me
up to my sense.

"But she will!! She will have a really happy life, without me
in it! You remember that day? I was partially insane and I
actually pushed her down bro! what hurts is that I didn't
care that I pushed her down! I didn't even bother to find
out if she was hurt. I left on the ground that day. I can't live
with myself if I ever do that to her again."

"FUCKER!!! Let that go!!! You were not yourself, people
do all sorts of crazy shit when they are angry! listen to me!!!
Ask her to join a college in Bangalore!! I am sure that she
will. Maybe she was waiting for you to ask her about it. She
is the one shot you have at living a happy life. You son of
a bitch! You can't do it man!You think you are bad?? Even
I have done things that won't let me sleep at night. But I
still live! She is your only chance at a normal life!!! You even
understand me?? Blink twice if you heard me." Bharat was
annoyed.

"If I do it then, I will always be afraid that I deprived her of getting something she solely deserved in life. fucker I am broken man! I except that And she is my glue that is holding me together."

"See thank god!! You got back into your senses!! When I asked if you will do what's necessary in B'lore... I meant you, begging her to come along with you! Not the other way around... You gave me a heart attack!! Now lets get you your glue!" Bharat told me and walked towards his ride.

"No stop!! If she is with me.... Then she will always remain as my glue. She won't get a life that is of her quality. The purest and happiest...." I tried to make a reasonable protest, but I wanted Bharat to knock me out cold and I wanted to wake up with Amrita beside me.

"Are you fucking crazy!!! You know how people used to treat her here! Being with you is also her shot at a second chance..." Bharat pleaded me to change my mind.

"Eventually she will move on in life! Maybe it will take a year or few at max. But eventually she will meet someone that will sweep her off her feet and give her the kind of life which she deserves! A kind of life only with sunshine and rainbow." I brokedown and felt as though my head was spinning. I went on my knees.

"Don't get all poetic with me you bastard...... fuck it! I understand you..... But you do know that you are going to regret it a lot! You won't have a quality of life which is worth living. You will be forced to live everyday in her memory.

Take it from me! You are never going to move on in life! Even if you date the most sexiest women alive, you will do it for name sake. You will never move on! You are going to die everyday slowly and painfully.. You still like your choice?? you shit head!!" Bharat kept both his hands on his head and screamed at me.

"I will regret it every single day of my fucking life!! I agree with you man! I won't have a quality life. But she will!! She will eventually have a shot at living a really happy life and I can't take it away from her, if she comes along with me...... Her chances vanish." My head was spinning and I kept my hands on my head for support.

"If this is what you want... I have to agree with you, even though I feel like killing you now! I have to agree with you. Get your ass up! You got a train to catch." Bharat said and lifted me up.

He dropped me in the guest house and went to pick up Asif and said that he will meet me in the railway station. "will see you in an hour then!" he said and accelerated across the dark street.

I kept my baggage inside the compartment and was chatting with my friends. "kiran didn't come??" Asif asked Nashi, who was to pick him up. "He didn't even pick up my calls." Nashi replied and checked his phone again. "Bro you never told me, about what Akhil told you that day!" Bharat asked me curiously while, Asif was clicking some candid photos. "Lets just say it works on a principle that if our school reject our hall tickets, then it's a huge problem for the school and a lot of questioning will be asked. But if the student, themselves reject the hall ticket. Then we are the only one going to get fucked up. Because even our parents will think that we are stubborn to study, and cheap shit people like suresh appear like god in front of them. That's what happened to kiran. If only they realized that our CEO and princi have 20 different faces, Maybe things would have been different. One more thing our 2nd pre board was fixed, they only corrected our paper man. there was no way we could have passed it. Many lecturers who work in the college needlessly, are also involved in it." I said and looked at the three of them, looking at me with their eyes bulged out. "fuck that hell hole man. I have heard enough...... And your train is about to leave. So getting going fucker!!!!! And don't masterbate in a train's washroom." Bharat said and extended his handed out. "Waran, sorry about what happened in the evening man. I can't actually believe that you are leaving now." Asif told me and continued "Bey harami.. friendship from the first day to the last man.. how long was it??" "Approximately 720 days, it was an honour being with you man. All of you!! It was a once in a lifetime journey." I said and after another round of handshakes and hugs. It had come to this, the moment when I actually bid goodbye to Hubli and everyone there. "Don't forget us Waran!! I will come to Bangalore sometime." Asif told me while clicking the last group selfie of the night. "Bharat, please whenever you get time man. check on Amrita and deal with anyone who tries to take advantage of her in any way." I said while boarding the train. "Hey!! We are all here right. Nobody can harm my babhi (brother's wife)" Bharat replied me with a smile. I could see the signal turn green, the train blew the final horn before departing. "BBBBBBye bro!!!! take care.... For a change in life try to be happy." Bharat said and all the three of them waved at me. "Love you all!!! Brothers for life!!" I screamed at them as the train began to gather up the pace.

Three months later

I had got a text on fb from Amrita. But I couldn't see her pro pic, I always hated that site. It meant either the user had deactivated their account or the user had blocked you. I didn't know what was worse. Her message that read 'not hearing your voice is the hardest thing I have done. I know why you did those things that day, I hate you so much because of that!! But I also love you for what you did... As much as I want to keep this up it get's difficult for me and you to continue. It is better this way. Miss you so much... I love you so much mr. waran and I know you do too.' All that text from her did was make me more miserable. I missed those times, when I was in a all time low and she always helped me get back to my feet. I felt that the ground below my feet was crumbling down. The days passed like years, I was feed up with the routine. Every night was the same, Had countless sleepless nights. The withdrawal did not treat me well. I used to stay up late in the nights and start to think about the whole journey of 720 days. I would play it in all different versions in my head. And in every version I imagined. Things would not end well for me, if I did not have my angel with me. I started to feel broken again, I did not feel anything but the depression. I knew it was because of withdrawal process, but somewhere in the back of my mind I blamed Amrita for not being with me through it. I started to blame myself for letting her go that day. "Maybe I should have went back again and convinced her to join any reputed university in Bangalore..." I kept thinking to myself. I would get out of my house for a early morning jog to get a fresh breath of air. Bangalore had slowly started getting cold. I could notice that people had slipped into their sweat shirts and jackets. After the jog, I would clean my bike daily. I hardly cared about the appreance of my bike, back in Hubli. I always took extra care of the back seat. The short stubble on my face, started to grow into a beard. My regular spiky medium hair, turned into a wavy forest. That's precisely how my mom described it. Every Friday evening, I used to sit in the dark isolated corner of my apartments terrace, with a bottle of beer. And go through every picture of her with me. I always had a habbit of clicking a picture during the most memorable times of my life. I had clicked some pictures of me when I was high on crack, I always thought it was strange though. I started to hangout with my high school friends again. It made me forget about cocaine and her for sometime. Many times a day, I would roam through the city until my bike gets run out of gas. Sometimes I would park my ride, in a deserted street. And keep my hand on the back seat, and feel every memory I had of Amrita rushing back to me. Drinking did help me forget it all for the moment. But I realized that I like the feeling of keeping my hand on the back seat of my bike, were she had sit. That was the only real feeling I had of her. Bharat used to call me regularly to check on me. When I refused to take the last packet of coke he had, he warned me about the withdrawal and said that it won't treat me well.

"Waran!! The results are out…." Bharat said over the phone.

"some prank because I didn't call you guys for over three months?" I asked him, still half asleep.

"Fucker the results are out!!! wait up dude your result is still loading." There was seriousness in his voice, with a pinch of anxiety, it was the same tone he had while informing us about the preparatory exams.

"Dude for real???" I asked him a bit loud, too loud enough to catch my mom's attention. "the results are out????????" she asked me in anxiety, I could see that her mid day prayer started early. "yes" I nooded.

"Congrats bhai!! You passed…… you got good marks as well, but they fucked our internal marks…… All of our internal marks!" Bharat screamed from the other end of the phone. "told you it will not be that dramatic…. I thought of scaring you. But given the current condition, which is I am sure very bad condition that you are in. I thought I will just cut the crap. How is the withdrawal treating you? I feel like I am going mad here." It was the first time, that my mom actually saw a smile on my face after two years plus, she walked out of the room with tears of joy.

"It is fucking awful man….. Never felt so depressed in my whole life….. After about three months of crack free life.. I can sleep for six hours a night now..what about you?? And what about others result?? What about Asif?? Nashi and bhenchod what about you??" I asked him with excitement.

"Nashi got a distinction bey!!! and even yeahh I passed ok!! That motherfucker princi should see my marks now." Bharat's excitement was not going to die out any time soon. "and Asif is not picking up his call.... He is out with his bro, I will tell him to call you!! And Waran.... Amrita also got a distinction man!! be happy now at least. And I will call you later ok. I am Getting calls from Many relatives who I didn't know that even existed are calling me now." He said and hung up. After speaking over the phone with my proud dad and overjoyed sister. I had dozed of to sleep again, sleep is just a wonderful thing, that allows you to forget everything for a few hours. I always felt jealous for the people who could sleep in the afternoon as well as in the night. "I wonder what Amrita must be feeling now!!" I slept with a slight smile on my face. I knew I was not totally away from her.

"Yeah say!!!" I said receiving the call from Bharat. There was no reply from him for over twenty seconds, I could hear him panting. I was about to hang up.

"Kiran is in a hospital man!! Those motherfucking clowns made him do this...... He went head on into a speeding municipal corporation truck..Can you believe it? He may not make it!!! Fucking life man!!!! what right do they have to take away a life?? The person laying in that hospital bed is not kiran!! His enitre face has changed, its like his body is slowly roting away. I can see the skeletal outline of him, covered with pipes and huge machines around him. His mom is not speaking or ready to except the hard fact man. She even tried calling him continuesly, after seeing him in the hospital. His dad is putting on that brave face." Bharath was fuming in anger.

"Were are you now??? What is his condition? He is going to make it right?" I asked him and got up from my bed and rushed to the balcony.

"He is in a coma, the doctor said. It's a defense mechanism of the body to not feel the pain."

"I know what it fucking means!!! I mean what is his condition??" I stressed on the word 'condition'. All I wanted to know was wether he will make it or no.

"Nobody is telling anything. I WILL FUCKING BURN DOWN PRINCI AND SURESH. They murdered him! You should have seen the amount of blood he lost." There was dead silence for a few more seconds. I could clearly hear Bharat's footsteps. "Don't worry dude. That fucker will come back unscratched, he will make a full recovery."Bharat told me after a long pause. It was hard to hear Bharat's voice in the commotion.

"I know he will. Where are you know?"

"Just entered the street to hell. And now I am looking at the same place because of which he is there. But they are celebrating here bro!! Suresh got what he wanted, but missed out on his life's goal. These bastards never have a soul within them do they?? And you thought that we are bad?" Bharat asked me looking at the central jail from some distance, I could hear him sip some drink.

"Maybe someday they will pay? For what they did to us?? All of us?" Bharat asked me in a feeble voice, but I was sure that he knew the answer.

"Just keep me posted on Kiran's condition. That son of a bitch will make it!" I said and hung up.

It is only for two years they said. The two years will be turning point in life they said. But what happens to people like Waran, Asif, Bharat, kiran after the road ends they never say. We live in a country filled with culture and tradition they said. But we also live in a country where girls like my angel, that saved my hideous life, is seen as nothing more than a used product then a person, That they never say. Respect the teachers, they give you education! And eventually a good life they said. What should people like us do when, people like my Princi and CEO was actually a demon within that they failed to see, That they never say. Even as I am writing this, even as you are reading this line. Another Thiru waran, Bharat, Asif and kiran will be getting harassed in such educational institutions, across the country. They say this journey is for 720 days only. But is it? they say that in an imperfect life, we always find something good for our self........ But few are just not destined for it. As life is not a fairy tale. Maybe people like them live in a shade, the kind of shade they create for themselves..... Like living in the shade of a dark cloud.

****

Printed in the United States
By Bookmasters